♡ one

perfect

night

LORANE HOPKINS

TRYST
A CAYÉLLE IMPRINT

Cayélle Publishing/Tryst Imprint
Lancaster, California USA
www.CayellePublishing.com

Orders by U.S. trade bookstores and wholesalers, please contact Freadom Distribution at:
Freadom@Cayelle.com

Printed in the United States of America

Cover Art by Robin Ludwig Design, Inc.
Interior Design & Typesetting by Ampersand Bookery
Edited by Dr. Mekhala Spencer

Library of Congress Control Number: 2021943019

ISBN: 978-1-952404-70-2 [paperback]
ISBN: 978-1-952404-65-8 [ebook]

one

perfect

night

one

2016

*T*he Grand Hawaiian Hotel and Resort in Wailea, Maui, was as spectacular as advertised, a place that Cassidy Roark, at this point in her life, could only dream of staying at, if it hadn't been for the huge conference discount. The views from her luxurious room were breathtaking, the pool and restaurants were exquisite and white sand beaches abutted a warm blue ocean. One of her favorite features was a lounge that had one wall open to the sea, that had light breezes and the aroma of unnamed flowers.

The three-day conference had finally wrapped up, all that was left of the program was the closing banquet for The Interior Designers of America Association. Tomorrow she would be going home, back to the reality of being a struggling interior designer. She had recently opened her own business and although things were gradually picking up, she certainly wasn't at a point where she could afford things like vacations, let alone vacations in Hawaii.

Cassidy had managed to splurge on a beautiful Halston, little black dress. for the banquet and it fit her like a glove, hugging her curves, accentuating her figure in all the right places. She gave herself a final onceover in the bathroom mirror. Her black hair hung in voluminous curls down to the middle of her back, covering most of the backless portion of the fabulous dress. She'd applied her makeup to give her almost ice blue eyes the popular smoky effect, and her alabaster skin was radiant.

She was ready for the banquet, but the banquet wasn't quite ready for her, she still had at least forty-five minutes before the doors opened. "There's always the Grand Lounge," she said out loud, thinking about enjoying a cocktail in the open-air lanai until dinnertime. Grabbing her bag, she left her room and headed for the first floor.

Gray Griffin had spent the day viewing property on the island of Maui. He was deciding on the best location for the construction of his next luxury resort, in Hawaii or in Marbella, Spain. His decision hinged precisely on location, and so far, he really liked one piece of land he'd seen in Maui, as it had great views and was on the side of the island that he preferred. The only problem he saw was a need for better roads to reach the property. Road construction would add millions to a final cost, even without figuring in the additional time, always an expensive factor. If the land in Marbella had an adequate road system already in place, his decision would be greatly simplified.

After spending all day in an open-top Jeep with his project and construction managers, Gray went back to his penthouse suite at the hotel. He'd been planning to stay in tonight and order dinner from room service, as he was leaving early in the morning for Spain, but after showering and putting on clean clothes, he changed his mind. He loved Hawaii, its people and especially the state's easygoing atmosphere, something he so rarely got to enjoy these days. The almost frenetic pace he'd set himself, building new resorts during the past few years, had spared very little time for a social life. He'd thought about slowing down, to try to find a better balance between work and his practically nonexistent personal life, but some new project always came along. And then any idea of actually developing a relationship with someone of the female persuasion drifted from his mind just as soon as the first shovel of dirt was turned, and construction began. Maybe next year, he thought as he rode the elevator to the first floor.

Once in the lobby, Gray decided to go to the Grand Lounge and enjoy the sunset with a glass of wine before dining in the seafood restaurant. Maybe he *should* slow down some, he pondered as he walked into the lounge. Maybe he should find a nice woman, get married … but that was a problem … a big problem for him. As soon as he told anyone who he was, billionaire hotelier Gray Griffin, he saw dollar signs forming in their eyes. If he could just stay anonymous long enough to get to know someone, then maybe he could find that one special woman.

"I'd like a nice chardonnay," he told the bartender, as he scanned the room. The place was packed, and it took only a minute to see that there wasn't an available table. Since he didn't feel like hanging at the bar, he asked the bartender, "Are there open tables on the lanai?"

"I'm sorry, sir," the bartender said as he set a glass of white wine down in front of Gray. "We're so busy tonight that I've barely had time to wash glasses, let alone go outside and check the tables."

Gray lay some money on the bar. "That's okay, I'll check myself. So, what's going on anyway?"

"A conference," the man said. "Their closing banquet is tonight so everything should quieten down in another hour or so. They'll all be gone tomorrow."

Gray thanked the man and went outside where he immediately inhaled a huge breath of that incredible Hawaiian early evening air. It's so peaceful, he thought as his gaze swept the area, taking in the packed tables with beautiful people so clearly enjoying themselves and the stunningly beautiful flowering plants, the décor that was so distinctly Hawaiian. He drank it all in, while he searched for a place to sit, hoping he wouldn't have to go immediately to the restaurant. He'd really wanted to just sit and relax for a bit before dinner.

Then he saw it. There was one chair available and it was at the table of a gorgeous dark-haired woman. He stared at her as though benumbed. Then, to his delight, she lifted a hand and motioned him over. He moved like a robot, one foot ahead of the other, his eyes focused completely on the most beautiful woman he'd ever seen.

"You're welcome to sit here, if you'd like," she said when he reached her table. "I'll be leaving in a little while, and you'll have the table all to yourself."

Cassidy had gotten the last table available on the open patio of the Grand Lounge. It seemed everyone else attending her conference had the same idea about killing a little time, in a beautiful setting, before the banquet. She had ordered a light rum punch and was slowly sipping it when she saw an extremely handsome man appear on the lanai. He stood there, at the entrance, for a few moments looking around. At first, she thought he was looking for someone. And why wouldn't he be? Someone that good looking certainly wouldn't be in Hawaii alone. He had to be at least six foot three or four with dark sandy-blondee hair, a lean, muscular build, a square jaw with even facial features and light eyes, though from that distance, she couldn't quite make out their color. His clothes were obviously expensive and looked as if they were made specifically for him.

When his eyes landed on her empty chair, she realized that he'd been looking for a place to sit. Perhaps his wife or girlfriend would be joining him later? Maybe he was waiting for her to get ready for dinner? She could let him wait for an open table. After all, she and most of the others out there would be leaving in another twenty minutes or so, or she could be nice and offer him the empty chair across from her, thereby guaranteeing him a table. For her, the choice was simple. She invited him over. He smiled at her, a lovely, warm smile, she decided, as he pulled out the chair and sat down.

"Thank you," he said, "I didn't realize this place would be so busy tonight."

"It's the conference the hotel is hosting," she told him.

He nodded. "That's what the bartender said."

"The closing banquet is tonight and starts in about twenty minutes. Then we'll all be gone tomorrow," she offered with a smile.

"He told me that too, but then, I leave tomorrow also. One last night in paradise," he mused.

"It certainly is lovely here," she said, taking in a deep breath and savoring the mixed aromas of sand, surf, and flowers. "I wish someone would find a way to bottle the air here. I'd buy a case and take it home with me."

He smiled. "I think I'd buy two."

"Jensen, party of two," a young man in a white uniform said loudly, as he came out onto the patio. "Jensen?" He then came up to Cassidy and Gray. "Mr. and Mrs. Jensen?"

Gray and Cassidy looked at each other and said, "No" in unison.

"Pardon the intrusion," the young man said, before heading back inside. "Jensen," they heard again, but now it was coming from the lobby.

Cassidy got a silly grin on her face and a mischievous glint in her eye. "Maybe we should be the Jensens," she said.

Gray was surprised by her comment. "I beg your pardon?"

"What if the Jensens are doing something really fun? What if they've got reservations on a dinner cruise and their limo is here, or maybe they're getting a couple's massage and their masseuse is ready?" Cassidy always enjoyed being playful. Of course, she was usually with people she knew so she hoped this stranger wasn't offended.

Gray couldn't help but notice the sparkle in her lovely blue eyes, as she spoke of taking these people's places. Not only was she a drop-dead beauty, but she also had a sense of humor. At that moment, he was enchanted. "They could be going on a moonlight helicopter ride," he offered, playing along.

"Right, we could be missing out on something really great."

"With my luck, the real Jensens would walk in just as I got my clothes off," Gray said. "That could be embarrassing."

A picture began forming in Cassidy's mind of this incredible looking man lying on a massage table with nothing on but a small towel covering his backside. Her breath stopped in her throat over the sensual thought. She quickly picked up her drink and took a sip, hoping he hadn't caught on.

"Are you okay?" he asked, noticing that she'd seemed to be choking on something.

Her cheeks colored a bit, but since it was just starting to get dark, she hoped that he couldn't see the change. "I'm fine," she said. To change the subject, she asked, "Do you get to Hawaii often?"

"Not nearly as much as I'd like," he told her, looking into her beautiful blue eyes and lovely face again, thoroughly enjoying the view. "I never get tired of it. And maybe that's because I don't get here very often."

"Ah, a vicious circle," she commented, noticing now that he had gorgeous green eyes. A true, very dark green color, quite unusual in her opinion, and extremely attractive.

"Of my own making, I'm afraid," he said. "How about you? How many times have you been here?"

"This is actually my first time," she said with sigh. "And, unfortunately, I didn't get to do much outside of the conference, so I guess I'll just have to plan another trip back some day."

"I highly recommend that you do."

"It's so romantic here," she said almost to herself as she scanned the horizon of the ocean. "It would be great to be here with someone special."

"I suppose it would be," he said, thinking for the first time that he too wished he had someone special to share this with. "Next time you come you should bring your ... husband or boyfriend."

"If there's any such person, I'll do exactly that," she said, with a laugh.

"I find it hard to believe that someone so ... well ... beautiful as you are, doesn't have a man in her life," he said as he watched her full, pink lips curl into a smile showing just a hint of very white teeth. "In fact, I bet you have several men vying for your attention."

"And that would be a bet you would lose. I'm so very tired of the dating scene. It's really rough out there. It seems like anyone I meet these days wants something from me and it isn't my money!" Oh, Lord, she thought, way too much information! Why was she always spilling her guts like this? Maybe she should head for the banquet hall a little early or even go back to her room to wait. Anything but sit here with Mr. Gorgeous looking at her like she'd just—

"I know exactly what you mean," he said.

"What?" she asked, surprised.

"When you said you felt like anyone you meet wants something from you," he began. "I can relate to that, I tell you. I would love to spend an evening with someone with no preconceived notions or expectations. Does that make sense?"

"More than you know," she said. "I don't believe that person exists though. I mean, and this might be a slight exaggeration, but only a slight one. It's like the men I've been meeting lately want me to commit to going to bed with them before they'll commit to buying me dinner!"

Gray laughed at her description; he couldn't help it. "I'm not laughing at you, I'm laughing—"

"With me?"

"I'm laughing because I get just the opposite," he said. "No commitment, no anything! I can't even get a phone number without a marriage proposal."

Cassidy laughed then, too, a genuine almost belly laugh. "Are we a sorry pair or what?" she asked. "Two wonderful people like us with, shall we say, commitment issues?"

Gray couldn't believe how easy it was to talk to such a stunningly attractive woman, and he found himself wishing this was just the beginning of their time in Hawaii instead of it being the end. He would really like to know her better. But did she feel the same about him? There was only one way to find out, he thought, as a plan began to form in his mind, a rather outlandish plan and one that she would probably say no to.

"I've got an idea," he said. And now he had a glint in his eyes.

"What's that?"

"I'm alone tonight and I take it you are, too?" he said tentatively. "How about if you and I spend our last night in paradise together. And the one guarantee that I make is that I have absolutely no expectations. I don't expect anything from you. We just spend a pleasant evening together doing whatever we feel like doing … dinner, dancing or just sitting here talking. The only stipulation is that we both have to agree on whatever it is we decide to do. What do you say?"

Cassidy thought it over for a moment. On the one hand she had a banquet she should go to, as she had already paid for her ticket, not to mention the price she'd paid for the dress she was wearing. On the other hand, here was maybe the most handsome man she'd ever met asking her to spend the evening with him. "I don't even know your name," she said finally.

He nodded his understanding but telling her his real name could ruin everything. So far, she didn't seem to know who he was, and he would like to keep it that way at least for tonight. Then another idea popped into his head. "How about, we do like you said, and become the Jensens?"

"Meaning?" she asked, puzzled by his remark.

"We're both leaving tomorrow, going our separate ways," he began. "We'll probably never see each other again. If we know each other's real full names, there may be some temptation to look each other up and that could complicate our lives in ways that neither of us want. I'll give you my first name and you give me yours, and we'll use Jensen as our last."

She studied him for a few seconds. He seemed like a genuine, nice, clean cut, extremely handsome guy, and as she'd already noticed before, his clothes were not 'off the rack'. Somewhere in the back of her brain she heard a little voice that sounded remarkably like her best friend's telling her to go for it. "You need to be more spontaneous," she heard the voice saying. "You never get out anymore, all you do is work. Go and have some fun!" This time the voice sounded like her mother's. When her mother was still alive, she'd often tell her she needed to meet nice people and enjoy her life more. She smiled. "All right," she finally said. "Just answer me one question."

"What's that?" he asked.

"Do you have a wife somewhere that you haven't mentioned?"

He smiled and held up his naked left hand. "No, I definitely don't have one of those."

They finished their drinks and introduced themselves by their first names only. She found the name Gray unusual, but it definitely fit him. She told him to call her *Cass*, a nickname she'd picked up in high school.

"Would you like to get some dinner, Mrs. Jensen?" he asked, as they stood up.

"Definitely, Mr. Jensen," she responded with a dazzling smile. This could prove to be a lot of fun. She just hoped he meant what he said about no expectations! That would ruin their evening. Well, she just wouldn't allow him to walk her to her room. They could say their goodnights exactly where they met, the patio of the Grand Lounge.

He grabbed her hand and led her from the lanai to the front entrance of the hotel. "If you like fish tacos, I know just the place. We can walk to it from here."

"I love a good fish taco."

No more than a block away was a shopping area where local vendors had set up booths and food carts. Cassidy had been told that if she didn't do anything else in her free time, she should go there. Unfortunately, she hadn't had much free time from the many classes and lectures she'd attended, so she was excited to see it now.

Once they arrived at the Market, Gray led her to a booth called Maui's Fresh Catch. He ordered for the both of them and when their food came, he carried a tray filled with paper dishes to a wooden picnic table with benches. "You are going to think you've died and gone to heaven," he told her.

"Can't wait," she said, as she reached for one of the dishes. And as soon as she took her first bite, she knew what he meant. "Holy moly," she exclaimed. "This is fantastic! I wonder if they'd give me the recipe for this sauce."

"Better than anything you can get on the mainland," he said, relishing his first bite. He so seldom got to do things like this as he was usually schmoozing landowners and potential clients with high end dinners. And as he dug into his food, he marveled at how much she seemed to be enjoying this inexpensive if not simple meal. If he had told her that he was Gray Griffin of Griffin International, would she have even agreed to walk here, let alone eat this food?

After practically scarfing down their tacos, they spent the next thirty minutes shuffling from one booth to the next, looking at everything. There were so many fun and interesting things that Cassidy would have loved to spend another hour there, however, her feet started to hurt in her new strappy stilettos.

"I really hate to cut this short," she told Gray. "But these new shoes—"

"Say no more," he told her. "We'll just grab a cab."

But what he hailed wasn't exactly what Cassidy was expecting. "What on earth?" she asked as a Pedi-cab stopped on the curb.

"This is the only way to really see the island," Gray said. "Any objections?"

She laughed. "None whatsoever!"

The Pedi-cab took them all over Wailea and the driver pointed out many interesting things about the city, the nightlife, and the local attractions. He also took them on a moonlight ride down by the shore.

"It's not exactly a helicopter, Mrs. Jensen," Gray said.

Cassidy turned and looked directly into Gray's stunning green eyes. "No, Mr. Jensen it's not … it's better."

Gray felt his heart warming. How did he have the good fortune of meeting this incredible woman, he wondered? He grabbed her hand and laced his fingers through hers, resting them on his thigh. This evening was turning out better than he'd anticipated when he'd decided not to eat in his suite. And everything they'd done so far was simple, easy and didn't cost an arm and a leg. Would she still have agreed to a Pedi-cab ride if she'd known he could afford the helicopter ride hundreds of times over?

Cassidy could not believe how much she was enjoying herself, and with a total stranger! But even though she hadn't known him for very long, he didn't feel like a stranger. In fact, it felt like they'd known each other for years. No, she didn't know his last name and no, she didn't know what he did for a living or even where he lived, but he was so easy to be with and so very easy to talk to. How was this even possible? How was it possible that she felt more relaxed with Gray than she had after several dates with the last man she'd been involved with? Maybe it was the mere knowledge that after tonight they would never see each other again that allowed them to totally be themselves without consequence. Oh, wouldn't it be wonderful if she could figure out how to do this with everyone she met? All of those awkward moments that usually happen on a first date would never have to happen again.

"My turn," she said to Gray.

"Your turn for what?"

"I've been here four days and I haven't even dipped my toes in the ocean," she explained. "Mr. Jensen, I'd like to take a walk on the beach."

Gray could see that they were less than a quarter mile from the hotel where they'd met, so he asked the Pedi-cab driver to pull over. "We'll walk from here," he told the man, as he paid him.

"I should be paying for this," she told Gray. "You bought dinner."

He smiled. He hadn't had anyone offer to pay for anything in many years. "I've got it," he told her. "You just get those shoes off."

They were near one of the benches that lined the strand, the paved walking path that ran between the beach and the road. She went over, sat down and began removing her beautiful, black high-heeled sandals. Within seconds, Gray was sitting next to her, removing his shoes as well.

"Oh, Lord, that feels good," she said, as she pushed her bare feet into the sand edging the pavement.

"I don't think I've done this since I was a kid," he said without thinking.

Cassidy looked at the handsome man beside her on the bench. In one way he was so "normal" like the way he loved crispy fish tacos and laughing when he had sauce on his chin. Yet, like now with that statement and his beautiful clothes, he seemed like he came from a different world.

They stood up and lamented together about having to carry the shoes neither of them no longer wanted. Gray shoved his into the side pockets of his blazer, then took her sandals from her hands and tucked them into the back pockets of his trousers. "Best I can do on short notice," he said, with a grin so adorable she wished she could capture it on film and take it home with her.

How truly amazing this evening was, she thought, with a spurt of emotion that had she pursued it could have easily caused tears. But laughter, not tears, was obviously the emotion of this wonderful evening, and she was loving every moment, that she and Gray, whoever he was, were spending together. If nothing more ever came from their one-night stand, which was an honest label to pin on the few hours they'd been together, she would go home happy. And she knew that she would never be sorry she had missed the night's big dinner, the closing affair of the conference's program.

Putting such deep thoughts aside, she wound the short strap of her bag around her arm and pushed it up and over her shoulder. Then, with nothing in their hands, they laced their fingers together again and strolled barefoot down to the ocean. The moon was rising over the water and the lights were flickering along the paved strand. Hand in hand they walked into the surf, the shallow leavings of the last wave as it returned to the sea. Another followed almost immediately, but laughing together, they lurched sideways to avoid getting totally wet. Up to their ankles was fun, but neither was ready for a real dunking. Cassidy couldn't help but wonder if Gray's trousers weren't getting wet along the hemline but ignored an urge to caution him about it, afraid she might spoil the mood and their fun.

After a few minutes of laughing and ducking waves, they fell silent without breaking their hold on the other. Gray sighed audibly. "It's pure heaven, isn't it?"

"That's the word, all right. I wonder why I never discovered this heavenly place before now. And why doesn't everyone living anywhere else in this big old world move here?"

Gray's laughter rang out, a booming, echoing sound that challenged the salty sea breezes scenting the evening air. "Imagine if everyone in the world did move here. It would be pretty crowded."

Loving the almost musical sound of his laugh, Cassidy joined in with her own laughter. It was such fun to be walking along and laughing with a friend, with a man so handsome and charming she could hardly believe her good fortune! Just imagine that, she thought while sopping up a tear that her hearty laughter had brought about. "You're right," she declared. "I guess taking a walk like this would be next to impossible."

He looked at her, all but piercing her gaze with his own and smiled. He swung their locked hands back and forth as they splashed through the slightly rolling surf. "I love this place … and I'm having a really wonderful time tonight," he said, in a much quieter voice.

Cassidy slanted him an inquisitive look. Apparently, he, too, was feeling the magic of their evening, maybe even as much as she was. Could they keep on with their little charade, never knowing each other's full name or any of the facts of life that made every person unique? Maybe he could, maybe he couldn't, but she vowed then and there that she would not be the one to break the pact they'd made. But deep inside of herself she couldn't help hoping that he would not only break the pact, but he would also crush it to smithereens. And that was the thought that brought a smile to her rosy lips. Looking forward now, she saw the top floors of the hotel where she was staying had lit up. They created a lovely skyline above the slightly swaying palm trees between the beach and hotel grounds.

"Oh, there's, uh, home," she said, wishing at once that she'd kept quiet about it.

"Ready to go in?" he asked.

She drew a breath, again wishing she'd said nothing. "Where is that wonderful music coming from?" she said, turning her head to look around for the source of the beautifully haunting Hawaiian music drifting on the night air while completely ignoring his question.

Gray also looked for it and he decided it was coming from the other side of a particularly dense stand of coconut palms. "I think it's back there," he told Cassidy, nodding his head in the right direction. He then turned to her, face to face. "Would you like to dance?"

She was a little bewildered at first. Was he asking her to leave the beach and go dancing somewhere or did he mean … "Here?" she asked.

"There's no law against dancing on the beach, is there?"

"None that I've heard of," she managed to say, noticing the ragged quality of her own voice. Gray was doing things to her libido, that just might have been dormant for a while. *Quite* a while, she amended as a little voice reminded her that her last meaningful relationship had died a rather painful death at least two years ago. And that really might have been her one and only meaningful relationship, she couldn't help adding, all within the privacy of her own mind. Actually, she was trying to push all of those unimportant images far away so she could think about dancing on the beach with this fabulous man.

And then he led her higher on the beach, leaving the surf behind, and assumed a traditional dancing position, his left hand inviting her right while his right rested lightly on her shoulder. She stepped closer to him, realizing once again how tall he was, tall and incredibly handsome. In all of her adult life she had never known a man to compare.

He began moving, slowly and remarkably surely, considering the sand they were on, she followed as easily as if they were on a dancefloor. She had always loved to dance and this one would certainly be one to remember forever, a memory to take out and savor when she was alone and maybe a little bit lonely. It didn't surprise her when his right hand slid from her shoulder to her back and then, of course, he encountered bare skin because of the design of her dress. She jumped a bit because his touch on her naked back brought life to every cell in her body.

"Are we all right?" he questioned, with tender curiosity in his voice.

"We are ... more than all right," she returned, and took another step closer to him, bringing most of their bodies in contact. "That music," she said dreamily, laying her cheek on his chest, precisely on the section of his stunning white shirt that was visible between the lapels of his jacket. He smelled divine and she inhaled deeply.

The dance went on, in time with the enchanting music that seemed to surround them, as well as the sweet sound of the ocean swells. The combination was intoxicating, and Cassidy kept snuggling closer and closer to her entrancing partner. He inched closer to her as well, and then, just as the captivating music came to a close, he placed his fingers under her chin and raised her face to meet his, in a kiss.

She didn't pull back, she didn't turn her head, she parted her lips just enough to invite his tongue to dance with hers. And they stood in that magical setting, with the ocean their only accompaniment and clung to each other, lips joined in the most delicious kisses Cassidy had ever been part of, and when he raised his head enough to take in a breath of air, she smiled at him and didn't try to hide the emotions she knew were filling her eyes.

"Is the Grand Hawaiian your hotel?" he asked, in a rough and husky tone.

"Yes," she whispered.

"Shall we go in?"

"Yes," she answered, forgetting all about her vow to say their goodnights on the Grand Lounge patio.

Arm in arm, they made their way through the loose beach sand to the strand, and then stopped at the closest bench, where they sat to put on their shoes. Cassidy was brushing sand from her feet when she heard, "Oh, oh, I lost one of your shoes."

Her mood was so in tune with the glorious evening they'd enjoyed together that she smiled and said, "That's all right. I don't mind walking into the hotel barefoot. And I bet it won't be the first time someone has walked in without shoes."

He chuckled lightly. "I'm sure you're right, but you won't have to do any walking. This is my fault and I take full responsibility."

A bit puzzled over that remark, she watched him don his own shoes. She felt so mellow that when he stood up and held out his hand, she laid hers into it and happily let him pull her up. But he didn't stop when she was upright, he bent a little and swept her up and off the walkway. In his arms, she felt ten feet tall, miles from the ground and she couldn't help but laugh.

"You are wonderful," he told her, sounding as though he truly meant it, and began walking to the hotel's entrance. She snuggled into his broad chest and happily inhaled his unique smell.

"I love your cologne," she said, as his long legs ate up the distance. "What is it?"

"Don't use cologne," he said. "You must be smelling soap."

"Well, it's wonderful."

"You're what's wonderful." He strolled into the hotel whose large doors had opened automatically at their approach. "What floor are you on?"

She sighed with genuine delight. "The fourth."

"Do you have your keycard?"

"In my bag." It was still wound around her shoulder, nesting in her armpit.

Gray crossed the lobby and Cassidy smiled at the few people looking at them curiously as they passed by. "They think we're odd," she whispered to Gray.

"No, they think we're newlyweds."

She blinked in surprise. "You could be right."

"Okay, here's the elevator."

"You must be getting tired. Let me stand for the ride up. It's empty and I really wouldn't care if it weren't."

"Neither would I." He let her feet slide to the floor of the elevator and pushed the button for the fourth floor. The second the door closed he pulled her into his arms again and kissed her with the same passion they had experienced on the beach. When the bell announced their arrival on four, he looked into her eyes. "Cass, you truly are wonderful. If only …"

The door swooshed open, halting whatever he was going to say, and she felt a heavy stab of disappointment. She wanted to know what would have come after *if only*, if only that damn door hadn't opened when it did!

They stepped from the elevator. "What's your room number?" he asked.

She told him, and they walked arm in arm down the hall. At her door, she lifted her chin in invitation. "Kiss me again," she whispered.

"Invite me in."

She studied the emotion in his gorgeous green eyes and knew exactly what he was thinking. After sucking in a deep breath, she whispered, "You're invited."

She awoke to the signs of early morning coming in through the balcony slider they left opened last night, because they weren't quite done enjoying the ocean breeze. The bed next to her was empty, she was alone.

But then she heard faint sounds, little noises that came from the bathroom. He was still there; Gray was still in the suite. She brushed hair from her face and eyes and wished she had risen before Gray, so she could have done something with makeup, or at least with her toothbrush. The bathroom door opened and she shut her eyes, peeking only when, by sound alone, she placed him tiptoeing from the bathroom to the chair not far from the bed. He was putting on his shoes.

Then he saw her. "Good morning," he said, with a smile so broad and beautiful she felt it rocket through her entire system as piercing as a lightning bolt.

"Good morning," she responded, and tucked the sheet a little higher over her breasts.

He stood up and took the few steps to the bed, where he sat down and leaned over her. "I have to go," were his first words. "I think I told you last night about my early flight to Europe."

"Yes, I remember." His eyes were even greener in the morning light and so full of intelligence and emotion and everything good that she couldn't stop staring. She dampened her dry lips with the tip of her tongue. "I'll be leaving this morning, too, just not as early as you."

He nodded as he looked into her beautiful blue eyes one last time. When he'd woken up that morning the first thought on his mind was asking her who she really was and where she lived. He wanted to see her again and again and again. But what if she lived in Florida or Chicago or somewhere else equally inconvenient for him and his work? Would a long-distance relationship work? And if not, then what? Would, or could she move to suit him? Did he have the right to even ask her to? Too many questions and definitely not enough time to answer even one of them.

"Damn, I've got to get going. My plane is probably warming up and here I'm sitting."

She nodded. "I understand, Gray." But did she really, she wondered. What she actually wanted to say was that their night together had been magical and that she didn't want to abide by their agreement. She wanted to know his full name. She wanted to know what he did for a living and where he lived. She wanted …

He stared at her for a moment. "Cass, you are one special woman, and I will never forget you, or last night."

"Same here, every word," she said, hoarsely with tears threatening her eyes.

He took a breath and kissed her one last time. "Thank you … thank you for one perfect night."

two

FOUR YEARS LATER

"Mama!"

Cassidy swept up the beautiful, sandy-haired boy in her arms and started kissing his soft cheek, ear, and neck. "I'm going to eat you up," she said between kisses.

"No, Mama, don't eat me," the little guy said, all the while giggling with each kiss that she planted on him.

Cassidy gave him one final kiss and then sat down with him on her lap on the couch of their suburban home in South Seattle, Washington. "Tell Mama what you're going to do today," she said.

"Ahhh, go to park?"

"What else?"

"Ahhh, eat cheese?"

"What else?"

This was a daily ritual for Cassidy Roark and her three-year-old son, Jaxon. Every morning before she went off to her office in downtown Seattle, and after he was dressed, Jaxon would come running up the hall to see her off. His nanny would, of course, be hot on his heels but would stand back and wait as mother and son bonded.

Caroline, Jaxon's live-in nanny, was an absolute godsend and the primary factor that allowed Cassidy to work, not to mention write her new book. She was working on a second book after the popularity of her first "Making Your Space Yours" had far exceeded her hopes and expectations in sales and public affirmation. It was about the psychology of designing and decorating one's home or office, and much more.

Over the last three years, Cassidy's interior design business had taken off and she attributed that success to her unique way of uncovering what a client liked and really wanted. After meeting with a new client, she would insist that they not see or speak with her again for at least a week. Instead, the client was to make a list of color preferences and take pictures of anything that caught their eye during that week. She explained to her client that they should take pictures of clothes in store windows, furnishings in hotels and even friend's homes, also artworks like statues, paintings, and pottery. Cassidy would then review those notes and pictures, and create a unique design using the client's own favored colors, textures, and patterns. So far, her approach made her the most sought-after designer in all of Seattle. Her book, using the same concepts, and teaching people how to use them, was making her sought after, worldwide.

"Do you know how much Mama loves you?" Cassidy cooed in her son's ear as she hugged him again. "I love you to the moon and back and then some."

"Love you, Mama," Jaxon replied, in his adorable singsong way.

Cassidy's heart melted at those three simple words. How on earth had she even existed on this planet before he came along? Her heart swelled as she looked into his gorgeous green eyes, eyes that looked exactly like his father's. "One perfect night," she whispered. "And now, one perfect child."

Cassidy made sure that her schedule was flexible enough to allow time every morning with this little bundle of energy. She also insisted that she be home with him every night and while there were occasions that required spending an evening with a client, she tried to make sure it was no more than once a week. The rest of the week she was home, having dinner with Jaxon and tucking him in at bedtime. And if someone didn't like that, they could find another interior decorator, as far as she was concerned. So far, she'd only lost one client because of her rule and that was an egotistical male that clearly had more on his mind than just redecorating his office. She hadn't been sorry to see him go.

The one area of her life that did suffer from her stringent rules was her social life, which, getting down to basics was pretty much nonexistent. That really didn't trouble her, though, as she was happily focused on Jaxon and her business, in that exact order. She didn't have time for dating and quite frankly, she didn't miss it. Her small circle of friends understood her priorities and accepted that she would not attend anything that interfered with her routines and Jaxon. And whenever possible, weekends were spent at parks, the beach or some other kid friendly place or event.

"Give Mama one more hug," she told her son. That was Caroline's cue to come over and take Jaxon from her lap. "Have fun with Caroline today," she said, as the nanny led her son to the kitchen for his breakfast.

Cassidy sighed as she stood up and went to the mirror in the foyer. There, she applied the lipstick that she didn't want to get all over Jaxon every morning. She fluffed her shoulder-length hair a bit and made a face at her reflection at the same time. The days, actually, the years, when the length of her thick, heavy hair reached the middle of her back were long gone. She had always deemed her hair to be her best feature, and now it was much shorter out of necessity. She had loved it extra-long but at seven months pregnant she'd been clumsy and weary, and it had become a hard-to-keep-up chore that she had gradually, if a bit painfully, decided had to go. She'd started looking for Seattle's most sought-after stylist, as only the best would do when it came to her raven locks. At his salon she'd fought tears as he cut, following her emotional instructions to take off only so much and keep it long but ... shorter. He'd laughed, she remembered, but he'd done an incredible job, and now she saw him every two months without fail.

She stared into her own blue eyes, which she always took pains to accentuate with the right makeup. Today she had used a combination of light tans and creams. Her outfit was a charcoal pantsuit with ivory piping around the lapels of the jacket. She always tried to look her best, and while she would never get past her love for the long, long hair of the past, it was now stylishly arranged, framing her face with slightly turned-under ends resting on her shoulders. It would have to do.

"Bye, Caroline, bye-bye sweetie pie," she called, as she put on her coat and opened the door. This had to be the hardest part of her entire life. Every single day she had to leave Jaxon and every single day she felt what could only be described as a sharp pain in her heart, along with a mountain of guilt that she had never been able to weaken into a molehill no matter how many commonsense arguments she laid on herself.

"Bye, Mommy," Jaxon called out. She walked out of her house while inhaling a big breath, merely another attempt to dispel guilt. She wondered, as she often did, how she was going to handle the day he left for college.

The drive to her office was especially tedious this morning, as somewhere in the vast sea of cars that lay ahead of her on the freeway, had been an accident. Luckily, she was near her exit. And once she was able to get off the freeway, it only took another ten minutes before she arrived at the beautiful, mostly glass structure she'd privately labeled *Cass's Cozy Corner*, which made little sense, since the nearest corner was half a block away but seemed to somehow make the building a little more hers, than it technically was. She was renting now but was hoping that by next year she would be able to buy it.

As she entered through the front doors, Cassidy could see the three talented young designers she employed to assist her as well as her secretary and the two women who kept her records up to date. "Good morning," she called out.

"Good morning," was called back to her from every corner of the building. Each designer had their own corner desk and workspace and the two bookkeepers worked in a shared space along the back wall. Cassidy was the only one with a private office and her secretary sat just outside her door. She did have one other room with a door and that was a large conference room on the south end of the building. This was all on the first floor, and though there was a second, it had never been completely finished by the builder. She had plans for that floor when the building was all hers and could easily envision a large design studio up there.

"Here are your messages," Diane said, handing her a stack of little pink notepapers. "You have a lunch meeting at 12:30 p.m. with Roger Hornsby and a potential new client, a David Wainright, is coming in at three."

"Where is the lunch meeting?" Cassidy asked.

"I'll give you three guesses and the first two don't count."

Cassidy laughed. "That man is so ... so ... what's the word I'm looking for here?"

"Predictable? Boring?" Diane offered, in teasing tone.

"That too," Cassidy said, as she walked into her office. "And if he didn't own an entire office building that needed serious redecorating, I'd skip the lunch. Oh, who is David Wainright?"

"I was wondering when you were going to land on that," Diane said with a laugh. She got up from her desk, walked over and stood in the doorway of Cassidy's office. "Apparently, he works for Griffin International."

"No kidding? Griffin International?" Cassidy was duly impressed. Griffin International was one of the biggest hotel/resort developers in the world, if not the biggest. "Did he say what he wanted?"

"Nope, just said he'd like to procure a meeting with you as soon as possible. That was his word, procure. Who talks like that?"

"People with an education," someone called out from another part of the room.

"Thanks, Diane," Cassidy said, with a big smile. She did enjoy her staff, and this was one of those moments. But it was time to get the day started. "And please remind me about thirty minutes before I need to leave for lunch."

After removing her coat and dropping her purse into a desk drawer, Cassidy started going through her telephone messages. She looked at the same message for at least a minute when she realized her mind was on something else, Griffin International. This would be a very big coup for her if she could land their account. They had resorts all over the world! If her work could be seen worldwide the sky would be the limit for her and her small business.

She pondered that delightful image for a few more minutes before she finally decided she had to do some actual work.

Cassidy had cleared her desk and was checking email when someone rapped lightly on her closed door. "Come in," she called out.

"Mr. Wainright is here," Diane told her.

"Please bring him in."

Diane took a step back and then re-entered with a tall, handsome, dark-haired man. Cassidy stood up and extended her right hand. "Hi," she said. "I'm Cassidy Roark."

The man took her hand. "David Wainright."

"Please sit down," Cassidy said, gesturing at a chair. "Can we offer you a beverage? We have bottled water, a variety of soft drinks as well as coffee and tea."

"Just some water," David Wainright said.

"Two waters," Cassidy told Diane. She had learned a long time ago that if she drank the same thing as her client, it put them more at ease. "Now, what can I do for you, Mr. Wainright?"

"You can start by calling me David," he told her.

"And please call me Cassidy," she replied with a welcoming smile.

"I'm with Griffin International, a hotel/resort developer," he began. "I hope you've heard of us."

"Of course, I've heard of you," Cassidy said. "I don't think there's anyone in the decorating business that hasn't. Actually, I don't think there are many people in the world who haven't heard of Griffin International."

"And I don't think there's anyone in Seattle who hasn't heard of Cassidy Roark," David replied, with a charming smile.

Just then Diane entered with a tray. On it were two glasses of ice, two bottles of water and a small bowl of lemon slices. "Please let me know if you need anything else," she said, as she deposited the tray on a clear section of Cassidy's desk.

"Thank you, Diane," she replied, as Diane backed out of the room. "And I'm sure you're being too kind," she said to David.

"Not at all," he returned. "The one name that kept coming up over and over again when I began inquiring about interior decorators was yours. And then I ran into your book, read it and knew why."

Cassidy blushed. She hadn't quite gotten used to the attention her book drew. "Thank you," was all she could think of to say.

"I'll get right to the point, Cassidy. Griffin International would like you to decorate the six hotels we've just acquired here on the west coast," he stated. "If all goes well with them, and from what I've seen in your book I can't imagine that it wouldn't, I'm sure we'll be offering more work."

"That's very flattering," she said, astounding herself by sounding normal when she felt as though her blood was now racing through her veins. "And I'd love to do it. I do have one question though, why doesn't Griffin International have a staff decorator? I would think a company as large and busy as yours would have a full-time designer."

He smiled. "We did. We just lost her in Spain."

Cassidy frowned. "Lost her? I hope not because of something … uh … an accident or …"

"Not at all. Forgive my poor choice of words," he said with a laugh. "She met the love of her life in Spain and married about two weeks ago."

"Whew," Cassidy said. "That makes me feel better. Now tell me about these six hotels. Are they being completely remodeled or just redecorated?"

Cassidy spent the next hour with David going over the specifics of this delectable Griffin International project that appeared to have just ended up in her lap. It was difficult to conceal her excitement but she somehow managed to appear businesslike and adult when what she really wanted to do was jump up and down and scream the way Jaxon did when she told him they were going to get ice cream.

The story from David was after an extensive stay in Spain, building four new hotel/resorts on the Spanish Riviera. The company discovered a small chain of six hotels back in the USA. And while the hotels were already built and in really great locations, they needed extensive remodeling and redecorating to bring them up to Griffin International standards. In fact, golf courses would be built, lavish spas would be added and even a full water park at one of them would be constructed.

"You see, each one will have a theme," David explained.

"It all sounds incredible. I just hope I'm up to the challenge."

"If your book is an indication of what kind of work you do, I have no doubt that you are indeed up to the challenge."

Cassidy and David agreed to meet back at her office at 9:00 a.m. the following morning so they could tour the first hotel. It was just an hour north of the city and it would be the golf-themed resort. He wanted her to get a feel for the area and show her the blueprints for the new construction. He then wanted to take her back to the Griffin building to show her pictures of some of the company's previous projects so she could see the type of architecture and decorating that Mr. Griffin preferred. Finally, he would take her up to the penthouse office suite and introduce her to Mr. Griffin himself.

"So there really is a Mr. Griffin?" Cassidy asked, as she walked David to the front door. "I always assumed Griffin International was a conglomerate of sorts."

David laughed. "No, there really is a single entity and he oversees every aspect of a project. Not that he micromanages, he just basically keeps tabs on everything and either approves or disapproves whatever is put in front of him."

"Uh-oh, so he could disapprove of me."

"No, I already showed him some pics of your work and he liked what he saw," David said. "Meeting him is really just a formality. In fact, I'll be the one you communicate with and I'll be the one presenting your designs to him. Oh, and I'm not sure I mentioned this, but Mr. Griffin likes at least three different concepts for each space to choose from."

"That shouldn't be a problem," Cassidy said, still privately excited but also feeling positive that she could handle the Griffin challenge, which was how she was viewing this massive project. She then bid David farewell and watched as he got into his Mercedes and pulled out of the parking lot. When she turned around, every one of her staff was standing behind her.

"So?" Diane said anxiously. "What's the verdict?"

Cassidy wanted to tease and pretend she had no idea why everyone was standing there, but the broad smile on her face and the sparkle in her beautiful eyes gave her away completely. "We're in!" she exclaimed.

Cassidy was so excited about her new project that she barely slept that night. And working on her book after Jaxon went to bed was impossible. All she kept thinking about was, what a boost this would be for her company and the people who worked for her. This was a once in a lifetime opportunity, and she just hoped she didn't blow it somehow. *Remember, they came to you,* she kept telling herself as she tossed and turned throughout the night.

And when morning finally arrived, she was genuinely surprised that she felt as good as she did. As she showered and put on her makeup, she even hummed a little tune. She truly felt that this was going to be a great day.

The suit she picked out to wear was her favorite and one she usually saved for meetings with extra special new clients. The black Calvin Klein pencil skirt and houndstooth jacket fit perfectly, and always made her feel like a million bucks, which, psychologically, increased her self-confidence. Her black pumps were a little more high heeled than she would normally wear to view an existing project, but since she was meeting *the* Mr. Griffin of Griffin International that afternoon, she would suffer a little to make a better appearance and hopefully a better impression with the big man himself. She spent a little more time on her hair, but the style was so set with its perfect cut, she was more or less stuck with it, which wasn't a bad thing. Finished at last, she gave herself a final look over in the mirror and gave her image a thumbs up. She could do no more, even if looking her absolute best felt like a necessity today.

"Mama!" Jaxon said, as he ran up the hall.

"How's Mama's big boy?" she asked, as she picked him up.

"Good!"

They went through their routine as usual and when Caroline was taking Jaxon to the kitchen, Cassidy told her, "I might be a little late tonight. I'm meeting a new client."

"That's fine," Caroline said. "Should I go ahead and fix supper for Jaxon?"

Cassidy just hated not fixing dinner for her little man and she especially hated the possibility of not eating with him. "I'm not sure yet," she told the nanny. "Let me give you a call. I might not even be late but just in case, I wanted to let you know. I'm meeting with a new client and you know how those things can go."

"No problem, Cassidy," Caroline said. "I'll wait for your call." That's what was so great about Caroline; she was always upbeat and seemed to understand her employer's circumstances completely. Once again, Cassidy wondered where she would be today without her.

Cassidy made sure she was early this morning. She wanted to be waiting for David Wainright instead of the other way around. As she entered the building, she could see that her bookkeepers were there as well as two of her designers. The third designer came in right behind her. Diane was seated at her desk and promptly handed her a rather lengthy note.

"What's this?" Cassidy asked.

"Driving directions to the golf resort project for Griffin International."

"I don't understand. I was supposed to meet David here."

"Not anymore," Diane explained. "David called about ten minutes ago and asked if he could meet you at the project instead. He said he has something he absolutely has to do for Mr. Griffin before he can leave the office. He asked if you could be there by eleven so he can walk you through the hotel and talk a bit. He said he'll then take you to lunch and back to the Griffin building for your meeting with Mr. Griffin. He also said if you had questions you could call him on his cell phone. His number is at the bottom."

Cassidy was mildly annoyed. Surely this Mr. Griffin would, or should, understand that his assistant had set an important meeting for this morning. After all, this was for his company. "Probably a stodgy old gentleman who can't even get his own coffee," she muttered as she went into her office.

Cassidy arrived at the project site at exactly eleven o'clock and was impressed by what she saw taking place. The hotel itself had scaffolding running clear around the front of the building with what looked like an addition being added on the back. There were earth movers off in the distance toward the north that she guessed were clearing land for the new golf course. The whole area was located on the brim of a rocky cliff and had a magnificent view of Puget Sound.

"Cassidy, my apologies for having to rearrange our meeting," David said as he exited the building and walked over to her. "Please come inside and let me show you around."

"Is it safe?" she asked, noting the scaffolding above the door.

David laughed. "Perfectly safe, though I do suggest wearing one of these while we're inside." He then handed her a bright yellow hard hat and placed one on his own head. "Not that I expect anything to fall on us, but you can never be too careful at a construction site."

Cassidy put the hard hat on and followed David through the front door. Right inside a construction crew looked to be tearing down walls and doing something with electrical wiring. "This will be the grand entrance. The check-in desk will run along that wall," David said, pointing to the south wall of the building. "Over here will be the concierge desk and right next to it will be two desks where tee times can be set up on the spot. Mr. Griffin would like this area to be very relaxed with sofas, tables and lots of greenery."

Cassidy started snapping photos with her digital camera and was already forming pictures in her mind of what this could look like with subdued greens, lush golden-browns and creamy-tans. She would also use gold fixtures in subtle shapes of golf balls and tees. The desks and check-in counter would be rich, dark wood with gold insets and the overall look she was going for was art deco.

David continued the tour, showing her where the pro shop would be, as well as the two five-star restaurants that were being added. They couldn't go upstairs to see any of the rooms as too many walls and floors were being removed and replaced. The area they viewed last was going to be a lounge. "And over here, Mr. Griffin has insisted we put in a glass wall that can be opened up when weather permits. Of course, there will be a patio with tables and chairs where people can go outside to relax and enjoy the scenery."

Much of the wall had already been removed and Cassidy could see the stunning view of the ocean. It reminded her instantly of her visit to Hawaii. There too was an open-air lounge with a beautiful ocean view, she remembered with a pang that seemed to leap throughout her body. And though there wasn't any beach to be seen today, she could still feel the warm sand of Hawaii beneath her feet, the breeze blowing through her hair and a strong arm around her back. "One perfect night," she murmured.

"I beg your pardon?" David asked.

Cassidy flushed slightly at the memory heating her entire system. "I'm sorry," she told him. "It was nothing."

True to his word, David took her to a wonderful little restaurant in the area for a great lunch. They talked non-stop about the project and she mentioned some of the ideas she'd already gotten from their tour. He told her about their plans for the golf course and how they hoped that they could persuade the PGA to hold one of their tournaments there.

They finished their lunch around 1:30 p.m. and headed back to downtown Seattle, David in his car, Cassidy in hers. It only took an hour to reach the Griffin building and park in its ample garage.

"I have one of the conference rooms set up for us," David told Cassidy, as they walked from the garage to the offices. "I've got photos as well as the actual drawings and some fabrics and finished boards that were used by our previous designer to present ideas to Mr. Griffin. I think these items might be helpful for you to put together your own presentations, you know, just by seeing how he likes things done."

Cassidy nodded. She was used to difficult clients and it looked like Mr. Griffin was going to be no exception. Of course, with his reputation on the line every time one of his resorts opened, could she blame him?

She and David spent the next hour and a half going over work done by the firm's former decorator. It was all beautiful work and Cassidy could certainly see why that particular designer had been chosen.

"This was our last project in Spain," David told her as he showed her a large photograph of the finished resort.

"It's beautiful, it's all just beautiful," Cassidy said.

"Let me give Mr. Griffin a call and see if he is available now to meet you."

"All right, and if you don't mind, I'd like to make a call, as well."

"Not at all," he said. "Do you need privacy?"

"No, I just need to give my nanny a quick call to let her know to go ahead and fix supper for my son," she explained.

David smiled and left the room anyway to make his call. As usual, Cassidy hated to miss dinner with Jaxon but it was already a little after four so she was certain she would not be home in time. She would make sure, though, that she was there in plenty of time to see her son for an hour or so before she tucked him in for the night. She just hoped no one would want to go out to dinner, though she couldn't think of one good reason why they would, since she'd already been given the job. It wasn't like anyone needed to court the other for this particular business transaction, the transaction was basically complete.

"Hi Caroline, it's Cassidy," she said into her cell phone once the call had connected. "I'm probably not going to make it home in time."

"I'd be happy to fix him supper," Caroline said. "What were you going to make this evening?"

"Chicken enchiladas," Cassidy said. "They're already made. I put them together last night so all you have to do is pop them in the oven."

"Perfect."

Cassidy's call ended just as David walked back into the room. "Mr. Griffin is ready for us," he told her. She smiled and nodded and then got up and followed him to the elevators. As he pushed the button for the top floor, she found she was a little nervous. He's just another client, she told herself as they rode up in silence. But that wasn't exactly true; he was probably the most important client she'd had since the beginning of her career.

"Long ride," she said, trying to ease some of her own tension. "Is this entire building Griffin International?"

"No, Mr. Griffin does own the entire building, but he rents out several floors to various other businesses."

The elevator finally came to a halt and the doors slid open to a beautiful reception area. The floors were marble, the furniture was luxurious and along with a secretary's desk with a woman sitting there looking to be in her mid to late forties, there was a security station with a very big, armed man sitting at it right outside the elevator.

"Sam, this is Cassidy Roark," David told the security guard.

"Please spell your name for me," the man said, as he began writing in a small notebook. "And I'll need to see some identification."

"Oh, ah, sure," Cassidy said, wondering why this type of security was needed. She got out her wallet and handed him her driver's license.

The big man nodded as he handed Cassidy back her license. She and David headed to the secretary's desk outside two large, double doors. "He's expecting us," David said to the woman who was typing into a computer.

"Yes," she said, and went back to her work.

David opened one of the doors and Cassidy took a step inside the massive, beautifully decorated office. She quickly glanced around. To her right was a conference style table made of mahogany. There were also some chairs and sofas in shades of brown to match the table. Several large flat screen TVs hung in various parts of the room. To her left, a library, two stories tall, with a spiral staircase, at the end of one of the huge bookcases. Directly in front of her was a desk also made of mahogany, The entire wall running from the library to the conference area was glass. There were paintings and beautiful statues made of marble and other materials that she couldn't accurately identify, as well as live plants and trees scattered tastefully around. And there was a man standing with his back to her looking out the wall of glass.

Cassidy's breath caught in her throat as the man began to turn. He was tall and lean with dark sandy hair, a square jaw and even features. His clothes looked as though they were made for him, definitely not off the rack. He had light colored eyes but from the distance she was standing she couldn't make out their true color, only she knew exactly what color they were. In fact, she knew what his voice would sound like once he spoke and she knew what he would smell like once she was close enough. Mostly though, she knew what the touch of his hand felt like on her bare skin.

Before she knew it, David was standing by her side and he was the first to speak. "Cassidy Roark, I'd like you to meet Mr. Gray Griffin."

three

$\mathcal{G}$ ray wasn't accustomed to being shocked simply by the presence of someone standing in his office. But this someone was a person he actually never believed he'd see again, though he'd thought of her often over the years. In fact, he had pondered on more than one occasion hiring a private investigator, a man he'd used often for various things to find the lovely creature he'd met in Hawaii, the woman who had captivated him so completely. But the way they had left things when parting, their agreement to not interfere in each other's lives, had kept him from doing it. Now, here she stood in his office, looking even more beautiful than he remembered.

Now what, he wondered? At least four years had passed, and both of their lives had continued as normal, or so he assumed. Was she engaged or married? Was she happy at all to see him again? Or had she found out who he really was and planned this whole thing? And if she had, how would he feel about that? So many thoughts raced through his mind in the split second he had before he had to either acknowledge their previous meeting or act as if he had no idea who she was. He wished at that moment that he could read her mind, know what she was thinking. But he couldn't. Hell, he couldn't even read the look on her face, that exquisite face!

He stepped forward and held out his hand.

Cassidy felt certain she saw recognition in his gorgeous green eyes. How could he not know who she was after the night they'd spent together? That fabulous night in Hawaii where they had walked hand in hand and danced on the beach. There was also what happened afterwards in her room, and after the lovemaking, the way he'd held her in his arms all night long. But there was the agreement they'd made, that damnable agreement! The agreement she'd wanted so desperately to break in the morning when they both woke. She'd even thought about following him to the airport, but she was afraid she would destroy the beautiful spell that had been cast between them. And though she had ultimately accepted the lonely fact that she would never have him, she knew she would always have the memory of that incredible night, in more ways than one! After all, he was the father of her child.

Then he stepped forward and held out his hand. She searched his eyes as she too stepped forward and took it, deciding at that very moment that she would say nothing about their previous meeting until he did.

The soft, warm flesh of her hand pressed firmly against his, sending electricity up his arm and through his entire body as they stared into each other's eyes. "So good to … ah … meet you, Mrs. Roark," he said, hoping to be corrected.

"Please call me Cassidy," she said as calmly as she could, giving away nothing of her marital status. She did wonder though why he'd called her Mrs. Roark.

"Certainly," he said, trying to match her tone. "And I hope you'll call me Gray."

She nodded, and then, as they dropped hands, an awkward silence filled the room.

Finally, and thankfully, David spoke, "Cassidy already has some really great ideas for the golf resort, Gray. I think you'll be very pleased."

"I'm sure I will," he said, feeling somewhat choked by emotions that he somehow managed to keep from exploding into words he didn't feel he should share just then. But if not then, when?

Another silence ensued so Cassidy decided to break it this time, "I should be going," she said, her eyes never leaving Gray. "I'm sure you're a very busy man and I certainly don't want to keep you from anything important." She then turned to David. "Thank you so much for the tour and lunch."

"Certainly," he told her. "I'll walk you out."

"Ah, David," Gray said, as they turned to leave. "Will you please come and see me before you leave for the day? I … ah … have something I'd like to go over with you."

"Of course," David told his boss.

Cassidy's heart was in her throat as she and David rode the elevator down to the first level. She could feel tears threatening her eyes and her pulse was racing so fast that she thought she might pass out. Gray had said nothing of their previous time together, hell he didn't even acknowledge that he knew her! She could hardly breathe from the shock that still ebbed and flowed through her body. She looked over at David and he seemed oblivious to her condition which seemed utterly ridiculous as she was sure her heart was beating so hard that he must be able to hear it if not see it jumping out of her chest.

"You don't need to walk me to the garage," Cassidy said, once they'd reached the first floor. "I know my way from here." She just didn't know how much longer she could keep her composure.

David nodded. "All right then," he said. "Please call me if you have any questions or want to go back to the property for another look. I'm usually available early afternoons. Actually, you can call me anytime of the day you'd like. I believe you have my cell number as well as my office number."

"Yes, thank you, David," she said, with a forced smile.

Once safely in her car, Cassidy broke down. It started with the tears she'd been holding back but before long she was shaking and full-out bawling. Luckily, she had a box of tissues and a box of wipes in her car. They'd been placed there for the unexpected disasters that seemed to befall three-year-old kids, the spilled juice box, the ketchup that ended up in between fingers and the tears from the dropped ice cream cones. She had never thought when placing them on the floor of the back seat where Jaxon's car seat was, that she would be the one who needed them most. But as the tears rolled down her cheeks in what seemed like never-ending streams, needed them she did.

"How could he?" she moaned out loud. "He acted like he didn't even know who I am!" Then another thought occurred to her that gave her pause and caused the tears to all but dry up. Maybe this … this job offer was his idea? Maybe he'd had David out looking for her? "But why would that take four years?"

Cassidy pondered that possibility a while longer. Hadn't David said they'd been in Spain for the last several years? Would Gray have tried to find her if he'd known he was going to be out of the country for so long? Probably not, it wouldn't be practical for either of them. But, if this was his doing, shouldn't she be flattered? "Surely he would have to know that after four years I could be engaged or even married," she said under her breath. "For that matter, *he* could be engaged or married and maybe that's why he acted the way he did." Was this just a case of coincidence or happenstance? Or was this something more? Was this Gray's way of … getting in touch with her? It certainly didn't seem that way right now.

She blew her nose, dried her face, and started the car. She would need to rethink this whole situation, including working on any Griffin International projects.

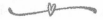

Gray sank into his chair as soon as the door was closed behind Cass and his assistant. He stared at the door for a good three minutes, half expecting the black-haired beauty to return, or was that internal ache merely wishing she would? Why hadn't she said anything about knowing him? But then, why hadn't he? He could have easily said something like, "Cass and I met a while ago in Hawaii. How have you been?" But he had been so stunned and tongue-tied by her presence and now she probably thought him a complete jerk. Which aptly described how he was feeling about himself.

He turned his swivel chair to face the windows. It had just started to rain. Grey clouds hung heavy over the city. This was a far cry from the views he'd had in Spain, of the beautiful blue Mediterranean Sea. Was he happier there? Should he have stayed longer? Truth be told, he hadn't been happy in quite a long time. If he was really going to be honest with himself, he hadn't been truly happy since that one perfect night in Hawaii.

Cass, or Cassidy as he now knew her, had made him feel special that night, she'd made him feel real, and she'd made him feel like a man. The bottom line was, she'd made him feel … period. And that wasn't something he could say about any other woman in his life. And that was because she was special, she was real. She had given herself so freely and completely to him that night in her room. A small groan escaped his lips as he thought about her beautiful milky-white skin, her full, voluptuous breasts, and her soft, silken thighs as she wrapped them around his shoulders.

He thought again about watching closely as she slipped out of her dress and stood before him with nothing on but a black lacey thong, with her luxurious hair cascading down in front of her, her erect nipples peeking out as her chest heaved a little with each labored breath she took. She had been just as excited as he'd been, and not ashamed to show it. Lord, she was sexy!

Gray felt his pulse speeding up and his breathing becoming increasingly more erratic as he pictured her lying on the bed, naked and beckoning him. She'd ran her hands up her body, from her hips to her breasts. He had removed his clothes as quickly as he could, and by that time he'd been so excited that he was nearly in pain. He had wanted nothing more than to be inside her, feeling her moisture envelope him, but he'd held off. First, he wanted to please her, in every way possible. He wanted to make sure they'd reach the same plateau of pleasure once their bodies became one.

He'd lain beside her and kissed her. He'd kissed her mouth, her cheeks, her ears and her neck. He'd kissed his way down to her shoulders, and then to her breasts, and beyond. And once he'd gotten exactly where he wanted to be, he'd kissed and suckled at her most sensitive parts.

Once he could feel the heat from her body rising, he knew she was almost there. He knew it was time to enter her. And when he had, when he started rocking inside of her, she matched his moves with precision. It didn't take long after that for them both to reach climax, their bodies stiffening and releasing at exactly the same moment. But that hadn't been the only time they'd made love that night … and each time was just as spectacular as the first.

Gray realized his eyes were closed and his body was reacting to his thoughts. He needed to stop this line of thinking and he needed to do it quickly. David would be back soon, and he certainly didn't want his assistant to see him in this condition.

He turned his chair back around and poured himself a glass of cold water from a pitcher that sat on his desk. What he really should be doing was pouring that glass on his lap.

"What did you want to go over with me, Gray?" David asked, as he re-entered the large office.

Gray had managed to calm himself down enough to talk without giving away his previous thoughts. "Actually, I just wanted to ask you a little more about Cassidy Roark," he said.

"Oh, what about her?"

"Tell me again how you found her."

"Sure, no problem," David said. "When you told me to find a new designer once we'd returned to Seattle, I started asking around about who was the best in town. And almost every person I asked told me about Cassidy. I also heard that she had written a book, so I bought it and discovered that her style and design philosophies are very similar to yours. Her book is where the pictures came from that I showed you before. Is there a problem with Cassidy?"

"No, no, not at all," Gray said, trying to sound nonchalant. "So, she didn't approach you?"

"No," David said. "I called her."

Gray smiled and nodded at his assistant. "All right, well, you can go home for the night. I'll be leaving soon too."

"Sir, if there's any kind of issue with her …"

Gray cleared his throat. "No issues," he said. "I was just curious as I had never heard of her before … but then, we have been out of the country for a while." Shut up, he told himself.

"I can show you the book she wrote, if you'd like," David said. "It's on my desk."

"Not necessary," Gray told the young man.

"There's a picture of her on the cover," David continued. "She sure is pretty."

"Yes, she's very attractive," Gray agreed.

David visibly sighed. "She sure is. And it's not just her looks, it's also her personality. She seems so full of life ... so open ..."

Gray found himself wanting to get up and slap the silly grin off his loyal assistant's face. "Is having her working for us going to be a problem for you?" Gray asked, probably a little too harshly.

"No, sir," David said, nearly jumping out of his skin. "I was just commenting on her ... I mean, I didn't mean it to be a problem, she's just ... you know ... I'm sorry, Gray, I will be professional, as always."

"Good," Gray said. And as his assistant left with his tail perceptibly between his legs, Gray found that he was actually angry at the young man who'd worked for him for the last six years. And in all of those years, there had never been a misstep. Had this been a misstep? Not really, Gray had to admit, once he'd thought it over. And what had David actually said? Anything that wasn't true? No. Anything that was derogatory or insulting in any way? No, definitely not, as that had been a hard and fast rule for any man working under the Griffin International banner, women would always be treated with respect, even if they weren't in the room. To Gray's knowledge David had never once crossed that line.

All David had said was that Cassidy Roark was pretty and had a great personality. As innocent as that was, it bothered Gray. Truth was he didn't want David or any male, for that matter, mentioning Cassidy in a personal context, not even for a compliment that she herself might appreciate.

And once Gray faced that fact he slumped in his chair. Even after four years, this woman still possessed a major piece of his heart.

By the time she pulled into her driveway, Cassidy had pulled herself together. The best medicine though was yet to come, and she could hardly wait until she opened the front door.

"Mama's home!" she heard a little voice shouting from down the hall. The next sound she heard was the pitter-patter of tiny bare feet slapping hardwood floors as Jaxon ran up the hall to greet her.

Cassidy quickly set her purse down and turned just in time to sweep her precious son up and into her arms. "How's Mama's big boy?" she asked.

"Good," the little one said as he wrapped his arms around her neck.

And that hug was all it took to change her mood completely. The sweet smell of her son and his high-pitched giggles as she kissed his cheeks was better medicine than anything else could ever be.

"Good evening, Cassidy," Caroline said.

"Hi, Caroline," Cassidy said, giving Jaxon one more kiss before setting him down so that she could remove her jacket and shoes.

"Stinky feet!" Jaxon said and then giggled and clapped his little hands together.

Cassidy laughed. "They probably are stinky," she said. "They've been cooped up in these shoes all day. Did you guys eat?" The last question was directed at Caroline.

"Yes, we just finished, I guess we should have waited a few more minutes."

"No, it's fine," Cassidy told her, picking up her shoes and purse. "If you have something you need to do, go ahead. I'm home for the night now."

Caroline was a live-in nanny, but she had family and friends that she liked to visit when she wasn't taking care of Jaxon. Her evenings were usually free as Cassidy routinely took full charge of her son once she was home. Caroline also had weekends off and would often go to stay with her single sister in Oceanside. And though they were both only in their forties, neither was married although both had been married at one time. Now, a widow and a divorcee, they fully enjoyed their single status and spending free time together.

"Actually, I might run to the mall," Caroline said. "I finished my book last night, so I need a new one. Do you want anything while I'm out?"

Cassidy looked down at Jaxon. "No, thank you," she said. "I have everything I need right here."

The rest of the evening was spent playing with her son, giving him a bath, putting him in clean pajamas and reading him a story. Cassidy hadn't had time to think about Gray or Griffin International or what she was going to do about either. Now that Jaxon was in bed and Caroline was in her room reading and she had the whole quiet house to herself, she couldn't stop thinking about both the man and the job.

"Oh, Lord," she whispered, as she plopped down on the couch. "What do I do now?"

On the one hand, she could call David in the morning and tell him that one of her best clients had offered her another job and she would be unable to do both at the same time. And since she hadn't actually started working for Griffin International yet, now would be the best time for her to bow out. She would of course wish him well and thank him profusely for the opportunity but in the end, it would be best for both parties. Telling her staff what she had done would be harder as she wouldn't want them to know her true reason for such a staggering turnabout, but she could come up with some logical explanation, couldn't she?

She lay her head back on a couch pillow and shut her eyes. What logical explanation could there be for passing on such a golden opportunity? "Especially since it's for Griffin," she whispered. A job like this one could be the springboard she'd dreamed of that would catapult her and her designers into fabulous careers. She'd been thinking of using one or two for each hotel, helping out herself with final designs and fabric choices. David had said they would require three presentations for each area to choose from. That would be a perfect opportunity to introduce her designers' ideas as well as her own. How could she take that away from her crew? Especially since her reason for doing so would be because she'd met a man once, and had a one-night stand?

She winced at the term one-night stand. But what else was it? And yet, look at the result of that one-night stand. "Oh,

Lordy," she whispered, taking back every negative thing she'd ever thought about that fabulous night on Hawaiian soil. Yes, she'd been reckless, and obviously, so had Mr. Gray Griffin. If either had used some commonsense along with some birth control, there would be no Jaxon.

And one more thing, maybe almost as important as Jaxon, although she wasn't sure that anything else ever could be, why should she crash the impetus of her career by refusing the biggest step up she would ever encounter because of one man? True, and maybe it was a little crazy to face, but the man who'd caused the situation was the same one who could make it worse. But if she refused the Griffin job, he wouldn't be making it worse, she would!

It was a mess and so emotionally troubling that Cassidy didn't know what to do next. She finally decided to make a stab at working on her new book. It was only a little before nine and she didn't usually go to bed until around eleven. She pulled herself up off the couch and headed for the den, where she'd set up a home office and studio. But after sitting and staring at her computer for thirty minutes and accomplishing absolutely nothing, she decided that working probably wasn't in the cards tonight. No, she really needed to settle in her mind what she was going to do, she knew that until she did, it would prey on her and push all other thoughts out.

"Damn you, Gray Griffin," she said under her breath, as she turned off the computer and switched off the lamp that sat on the corner of her desk. She didn't immediately get up though. Instead, she sat in the dark with only the light from the hallway dimly illuminating the room. "Why didn't I just mind my own business and go to the banquet that night in Hawaii?" she asked herself. But if she had done that, she wouldn't have Jaxon now and she would not, for all the tea in China, go back to living without that little munchkin, even if that were an option. It was the same painful circle of regret and thankfulness that she went through nearly every day, more than once today already and she had no doubt it would happen again before she slept.

If she were really going to face facts, all of the facts, she wouldn't take back anything about that night. It had truly been the perfect date, the perfect night, and no other relationship, short-lived, longer or otherwise, that she'd been part of could compare.

She shook her head in an attempt to stop the pictures that had started forming in her mind, pictures of the gorgeous man standing on the patio searching for a place to sit, then laughing and talking with him as they walked to get fish tacos. She then remembered how they rode around Wailea in a Pedi-cab and how he apologized for it not being a helicopter ride. Strolling hand in hand on the beach with that beautiful Hawaiian music playing off in the distance was pure heaven. Then when he'd put his arms around her to dance, she'd felt almost faint. But it was the kiss, that incredible first kiss that had sealed the deal. She knew the moment their lips touched, and their tongues intertwined in a hot, moist dance that she knew she was head over heels for him and nothing, not even the devil himself, could stop her from spending every last moment she could with him.

She felt her face flushing a little as she remembered their night in her room. She had already removed her dress and was lying on the bed when he began undressing in front of her. He was so lean and muscular with six pack abs and legs that looked as if they could run marathons. By the end of the night, she knew no one could ever say he didn't know how to please a woman. In fact, it was as if Gray had private lessons in the pleasing-a-woman department.

No, she wouldn't change a single thing about that night, at least not anything that had happened between them. But if she had to do it all over again, she would try to talk to him more in the morning, ask his real last name, ask if there was any way they could meet again, if for no other reason than to see if there was any chance for a relationship. He had seemed to care for her as much as she cared for him. He had even been clearly reluctant to leave her that morning. Oh, why hadn't she said something then? And why hadn't he?

Cassidy got up from her desk and padded down the hall to her room. As she passed Jaxon's room, she peeked in at him and saw a tiny foot outside the covers. She tiptoed in and carefully moved the adorable little foot back under the blankets. She then brushed his forehead with the palm of her hand. He was sleeping soundly, as children do, and would not remember this, but she would. She would remember this and hundreds of other moments like this for the rest of her life. She smiled and then bent down and kissed the top of his head before leaving and completing her journey to her own bedroom.

It was still early for her, only ten o'clock but she had a good book she would read to try and take her mind off her current circumstances. She had to decide whether to keep the Griffin International account, or not. But maybe if she slept on the problem a sensible solution would come to her by morning.

After removing her makeup and brushing her teeth and hair, Cassidy put on her favorite nightshirt and slipped in between the soft, cool sheets of her comfortable bed. She had arranged her pillows so that she could read but as she picked up her book, the pillows seemed to shift and bunch up. She tried rearranging them, but that didn't feel good either. She completely sat up on the edge of the bed and tried fixing them again. But as soon as she laid back, her neck started hurting and her shoulders felt like they had no support at all. What the heck was going on?

Cassidy finally gave up on reading and pushed all but one pillow to the other side of her bed. But try as she might, she still could not get comfortable. Something was causing her a great deal of distress. Was it just seeing Gray again today? Was it the thought of working with him, or for him, that had her feeling so uneasy? Was it his reaction, or rather non-reaction to seeing her standing in his office that had her so unnerved?

She got back up out of bed and went up the hall to the kitchen for a glass of water. On her way back to her bedroom she couldn't resist one more look at her reason for living. She stuck her head back into Jaxon's room and then, all at once, it hit her, with the force of a lightning bolt. With a dry mouth she grasped the reason for so many negative concerns, why this whole proposition was causing her so much distress. And it wasn't just seeing Gray again or even working for him. Hell, that could even be fun, if it wasn't for …

"Jaxon!" she said aloud. This little boy had a father, and he'd just walked back into their lives. "Oh, dear God," she whispered, as she went to her own room and crawled into bed. She felt physically ill.

As long as Gray was a distant memory, a man she'd always believed she would never lay eyes on again, she was fine with him not knowing he had a son. But now? Should she tell him?

How could she not? He had a right to know, didn't he? And once she'd told him, would he be happy about it? And if he was happy, would he want to be a part of Jaxon's life? Would he want to see him regularly, spend time with him? If so, he would also be a part of her life. How did she feel about that? But more importantly, what about Jaxon? He was still too young to understand that he had a father, but he would grow up and someday ask questions. She had always planned, if far off in the back of her mind, to tell him the basic truth, she had met a man and fallen in love, but it just hadn't been possible for them to be together. Now everything was different. If she didn't tell Gray about his son, she would have to lie to Jaxon, possibly even tell him that it was her decision to keep his father out of his life. Could she do that? Lie and lie and lie, and keep Jaxon from the truth, so help her God?

So, she decided, the choice was really no choice at all, she *had* to tell Gray about Jaxon. Not for Gray, but for his son, and so she wouldn't be burdened with lies for the rest of her life.

Then another thought occurred to her, and this one kept her awake until morning. What if Gray *did* want to know his son, and not just be a part of his life, but be a full-time father? He had the money and resources to go to court and gain full custody. Cassidy's heart sank as she wondered if he would ever do something that terrible. The truth, of course, was that she had absolutely no idea what Gray would do or say about anything, especially if and when he found out he had a son, and that was because she really had no idea who Gray Griffin really was. All she knew about him was that he was a fantastic lover, and fabulous on a first date.

There was one other thing that she now knew about him, that he had built a billion-dollar hotel-empire. And while she'd always believed Griffin International was some kind of conglomerate, she's just found out that it was one man, one obviously strong, smart man with a head for getting things done. And hadn't David told her that Gray watched over everything when it came to his business? Would he now insist on watching over his son in the same way?

Cassidy bolted out of bed and ran to her bathroom where she dry-heaved over the sink. When she finally stopped, she splashed cold water on her face and rinsed out her mouth with mouthwash. The only reason she hadn't heaved her guts out for real, she realized, was because she hadn't eaten any dinner. She knew she would've been a lot sicker if she had.

Cassidy looked at her image in the mirror. She looked pale and drawn and she knew that by morning she would have bags under her eyes. "And all because of one perfect night," she said with a heartbroken little sob.

Four

*J*ust as she had expected, Cassidy hadn't slept very well. Sure, she had dozed from time to time but during those times her head had been filled with nightmares. Mostly they were of losing Jaxon. In one dream, she'd lost him in a crowded shopping mall, and no one would help her find him. In another, she'd lost him in a snowstorm and there was no one around to help. In the third dream, she was at the beach with her baby, watching as the ocean currents carry him farther and farther out. She had no doubt about why this particular theme filled her dreams, but she didn't know how to stop her fears from surfacing while she slept, so she'd forced herself to be wide awake after each disturbing episode.

"Just don't tell him," she told herself sternly, once the clock finally reached 6:00 a.m. "What Gray doesn't know won't hurt him." But it would eventually hurt Jaxon and she knew that. She sighed as she dragged her exhausted body out of bed and to the bathroom. And once she got a good look at herself in the mirror, she knew she couldn't face anyone in public today. Her eyes were puffy and red-rimmed with enormous circles under them, her cheeks looked sunken and she simply could not force a smile to her lips no matter how hard she tried. And, last but not least, her stomach was still upset.

Cassidy knew Caroline would be up. The nanny was always up before her and had the coffee on by the time she made her way to the kitchen. Jaxon, on the other hand, would probably sleep another hour at least. She went to find Caroline to tell her that she wouldn't be leaving the house, and if she wanted, she could have the day off.

"Are you okay?" Caroline asked, obviously concerned as soon as she saw Cassidy.

"I'm not feeling very well," Cassidy told her. "I'm going to work from home today so feel free to go see your sister."

"If you're not well, I'll watch Jaxon so you can rest," Caroline offered.

"No, really, I'm just … I'll be fine … you go ahead, I'll watch him today." And maybe that was really all there was to her illness, she couldn't bear to leave her son. Yes, she was tired. Yes, she knew she looked awful. But not so long ago, when she was still footloose and fancy free, there had been days when she had managed to get to work on less sleep than she'd had last night. The thought of being away from Jaxon today though was just too much for her to handle.

"Okay, but you have my cell number," Caroline said, generous and concerned as always. "If you get to feeling worse, just give me a call and I'll head right home."

Cassidy nodded. "Thank you, Caroline."

As soon as she was gone, Cassidy called her office and left a message for Diane, letting her know she would be working from home and to call if something requiring her attention came up. Once that was done, she went to Jaxon's room. He was still sound asleep and looking like an angel. She went to his bed, sat on the edge of it and watched him breathe. He had just gotten his "big-boy" bed, but he looked so small in it this morning.

A tear slipped out of the corner of Cassidy's eye and down her cheek. She would fight tooth and nail for him—she would fight off a grizzly bear if need be. And she would fight Gray Griffin if it came to that. But would that ever be necessary? Her thoughts were so jumbled right now she didn't know what to think next. Before long, Cassidy was lying next to her son, holding one of his tiny hands. Within moments she was back in dreamland.

"Mama, Mama, wet."

Cassidy slowly opened her eyes. For a moment she didn't know where she was but as soon as Jaxon's little face came into view, she realized that she had fallen asleep in his bed. "What's the matter, sweetheart?" she asked.

"Wet," he repeated.

Jaxon was mostly potty trained, but he still had accidents at night, so he wore pull-up diapers under his jammies. Apparently, he'd had an accident last night. "Okay," Cassidy told her son. "Mommy will get you some clean clothes. But first, let's hit the bathroom and get you cleaned up."

Cassidy and Jaxon made their way to the bathroom after a quick stop in her room to retrieve her cell phone. Once she had Jaxon in the tub, she checked her phone for messages and was surprised to see the time; it was already after eight. She had really zonked out! And the thing was she could have easily slept a few more hours. She decided to call her office to make sure Diane had gotten her message and to see if she had any calls to return.

"Hey, Diane," she said, once the connection was made.

"Cassidy? Are you okay?" Diane asked, with genuine concern in her voice. Cassidy rarely missed a day at the office, although sometimes she would leave early and work from home, mostly due to Jaxon.

"I'm fine," Cassidy said. "I think I'm just exhausted."

"Of course, you are," Diane affirmed. "You've been burning the candle at both ends, what with being in the office all day and then trying to write another book at night after your son goes to bed. Something had to give eventually."

Cassidy had been pregnant when she'd written her first book, so her evenings had still been her own. "That's true," Cassidy agreed. "Anyway, I just called to see if I had messages that shouldn't be ignored, or if anyone there had questions that needed an answer from me."

"Don't worry about the office," Diane said. "Everything is humming right along here. You only have one message this morning and it was from the big man himself."

"Who is that?" Her heart nearly stopped, because she instinctively knew who the 'big man' was.

She was right, for Diane easily replied, "Mr. Gray Griffin."

Gray had tossed and turned all night. At first, he'd blamed his restlessness on the spicy Chinese food he'd eaten for dinner, but deep down he'd known that wasn't true. He ate that food often, stopping at his favorite Chinese restaurant on his way home from the office to his penthouse condo, and it had never kept him up before. But something had. Something had preyed on his mind and he had a sneaking suspicion that it had something to do with a stunningly beautiful woman named Cassidy Roark.

Seeing her again had made him painfully aware of how alone he was, especially since he was once again eating dinner by himself. He'd thought about scrapping the Chinese food and calling one of the many numbers he had in his little black book, but after flipping through several pages he realized that none of these women really appealed to him. Not the way Cassidy did.

After facing that jarring fact, sleep had basically been a lost cause.

When Gray finally gave up on sleep and got up at 5:20 a.m. he knew he had to do something about this unexpected twist of fate. Whether it was fate, karma or whatever, the woman who had haunted his dreams on and off for four years now was within reach, and it must mean something. He was not a man to let opportunity slip past him unexplored, and he felt especially driven to get to the bottom of this second meeting with Cass. Yes, Cass was how he thought of her, even though now he knew her full name, but Cass was the name attached to the most thrilling night of his life and to him, Cass she would remain.

The bottom line was, he had to find out if she was single and maybe more important, he had to know if the connection they'd made in Hawaii was strictly a magical one-night stand, or if there was any hope in hell of there ever being a relationship between them. The question was, how was he going to get his answers?

After making coffee and taking a long hot shower, Gray dressed for the day. He selected a tailored dark blue Armani suit with a white shirt and blue silk necktie. He always liked to look good, but an *ordinary good* wasn't enough, not if there was a possibility of seeing Cassidy today. He picked out one of his best suits, and as soon as he was dressed in his perfectly fitted clothes, he was out the door, on his way to the office, the place where he spent most of his time.

Would that change? he wondered, if he and Cassidy were together? Was he already thinking of a committed relationship with her? Dare he go that far when he was so in the dark about her personal life?

As he climbed behind the wheel of his Maserati Gran Turismo, he made a mental note to avoid mentioning any plans or hopes concerning Cassidy to David, not even subtle hints. He didn't need the young assistant asking questions, especially if it turned out that Cassidy was married or somehow otherwise taken. And if she wasn't, David would find out about the two of them soon enough if and when they started to see each other.

It was still very early, only around 6:30 a.m. The roads were practically clear, and it took Gray only twenty minutes to get to his office building. The night guard was still on duty, but he wasn't really surprised to see Gray, as the big boss was often there before the guard left for the night, and still there when he came back on shift in the morning.

"Good morning, Mr. Griffin," the man said, as Gray passed by the security desk in the lobby.

Gray nodded in the guard's direction but didn't stop to chat, as he often did. He was on a mission this morning, and he would not let anything waylay him. On his way in he'd thought about just looking Cassidy up on the internet himself, but he felt that the stories one found online these days were unreliable. Simply anyone could post just about anything they wanted, true or not. So, when he got to his office, he picked up his telephone and called the one person that he knew would not only be able to find out what he wanted to know, he would do it quickly and discreetly.

"Paul, Gray Griffin," he said, "I know it's early, but I need some information, and I need it ASAP." Paul Radley was a private investigator and someone Gray trusted implicitly. He had helped Gray when he needed a background check done on someone, whether it was a promising new employee, someone Gray was thinking of doing business with, or even a woman he was interested in dating. Gray left very little, if nothing to chance.

"What do you need, Gray?"

"All I want to know is if a woman named Cassidy Roark is married or engaged. She's an interior designer here in Seattle." He spelled Cassidy's name for the investigator.

"Do you want a full background done on her?" Paul asked.

Gray thought about that for a moment. He usually requested a thorough investigation be done on anyone he was interested in dating but somehow it just didn't seem right this time. What he really wanted was to find out things about her on his own, the way normal people did when they first meet someone. He wanted to spend long evenings getting to know her. He wanted to find out what her favorite food was all on his own, if she was single, that is. "No," he finally told Paul. "Just find out if she's married or involved."

"That should be easy," Paul said. "I'll get back to you within the hour."

And as always, Paul was true to his word. Gray had his answer in less than thirty minutes. Cassidy Roark was single and, in fact, not even currently dating. Gray waited until eight o'clock before he called the offices of Cassidy Roark and Company, Interior Designers.

Cassidy nearly swallowed her teeth. "Who?" she asked weakly.

"Gray Griffin," Diane repeated. "Of Griffin International."

Cassidy's stomach started doing flip-flops and her heart began racing. "Did he say what he wanted?" she asked, forcing herself to speak calmly.

"He wanted you to call him as soon as you got here," Diane explained. "Sounded urgent to me. But I told him you were working at home today, so then he asked me to pass on his message, and then repeated the importance of you returning his call as soon as possible. He left both his desk and cell phone numbers. I didn't tell him you weren't feeling well, but I could call him back and let him know you wouldn't be returning his call until tomorrow, if you'd like."

"Ah … no … text me his phone numbers as soon as we're off the line. I'm giving Jaxon a bath, and I don't want to leave him to get a pen," Cassidy said, with an almost painful sinking sensation.

"Will do," Diane said cheerfully.

As soon as the connection was broken, Cassidy's mind started to race. "He knows about Jaxon," Cassidy said, under her breath. But that wasn't possible so fast, was it? And even if he knew she had a child; he certainly had no way of knowing the child was his. That would take a DNA test. So, what did he want?

Cassidy moved to the edge of the tub and finished bathing her son. While she was drying him off, she heard the chime from her cell phone that indicated she had a text message. She knew that Gray's phone numbers were now within easy reach, and he wanted her to call him. She'd thought about this very thing so many times over the last four years and had come up with so many clever things to say if she ever saw him again. Now, she couldn't think of a single line she'd written so many times in her head. In fact, her mind was completely blank where he was concerned. Her stomach, on the other hand, was turning over and over and didn't contain just a few butterflies, but a whole herd of them.

After Jaxon was dried and dressed, Cassidy picked up her phone and looked at the text message. Diane had made it simple, two numbers, one for Gray's office and one for his cell phone. She bit her lip as she pondered on whether or not to take a few minutes now to call him.

"Hungy, Mama," Jaxon said.

Decision made. "What do you want for breakfast, sweetheart?" she asked. He always woke up hungry. "How about a pancake?"

"Yes!" Jaxon said, taking off in a run.

Cassidy followed her son to the kitchen where she spent the next hour making pancakes, eating them with Jaxon and then cleaning up the mess, all the while keeping one eye on her phone. She had set it on the table, telling herself that she had it with her because of work. But why keep staring at it as if it were going to break into a wild dance or something? After all, she was supposed to call him, not the other way around.

She sighed as she thought about just picking the damn thing up and getting it over with. But then it rang, causing her to nearly jump out of her skin. Caller ID indicated it was Diane.

"Hey, Di, what's up?" she asked, once she'd hit the little green button on her phone.

"Mrs. Fletcher just called," Diane told her. "She said, the venue for the rehearsal dinner of her daughter's wedding has just canceled, so she is going to have to host the affair at her home, and is there any way you can finish her living room before the 14th?"

"Wow that only gives me …" Cassidy did a quick calculation in her heard. "About six working days. I'm going to have to call the upholsterers, the painters and the place where we're getting the lighting fixtures manufactured. Luckily the new flooring went down two days ago. Tell you what, call Mrs. Fletcher back and tell her that I'll call her by the end of the day. Tell her what I'm doing, and … damn, I forgot about the area rugs. They're being hand-made, and they'll never be completed before the 14th. Have Jennifer run over to the Seattle Market and see if she can find something we can put down just for the dinner. The color scheme is in the file in my office. She won't have any trouble finding it."

"Will do," Diane said. "In the meantime, how are you feeling?"

"I'm fine," Cassidy said, but was she really? As long as she wasn't thinking about Gray she was fine but the second her thoughts turned back to him, she could barely breathe. "Really," she added for emphasis.

"Sorry to throw this at you while you're at home but Mrs. Fletcher sounded positively panic stricken."

"Mrs. Fletcher is always positively panic stricken," Cassidy said. "Actually, this will give me something to think about other than … my stomach."

Cassidy spent the next several hours on the phone with the vendors she was using for Mrs. Fletcher's *new* living room. And after pulling a few strings, calling in some favors and all but groveling, she'd finally been able to call Mrs. Fletcher to tell her that her room would indeed be done by the 14th, and she was able to make that call before the end of the day!

"Everything but the area rugs," Cassidy said. "But we'll get something in your color pallet for the dinner. I'm sure you'll be happy."

"Oh, Cassidy, you are a miracle worker!" Mrs. Fletcher gushed.

"I don't think I'd go quite that far," Cassidy said with a laugh.

"Hungy, Mama," Jaxon said, as soon as she was off the phone.

"Already? Well, let's see what we can find to eat." She was thinking of giving her son a snack but then saw what time it was. "Holy cow," she said, realizing that she'd completely lost track of time. "It's nearly one-thirty! No wonder you're hungry."

Cassidy made sandwiches and then sat at the table with her beautiful boy. He had been so good today while she was on the phone. He'd mostly played in his room which had allowed her the time and quiet she'd needed to work. He certainly deserved a special treat this afternoon for that. "How would you like Mama to take you to the park?"

"Yes!" he shouted. He loved the park, especially when the sun was shining like it was today. Seattle weather leaned toward clouds and rain, and sunshine was always appreciated.

"Okay, you finish your sandwich while Mama gets dressed." Cassidy could hardly believe it was almost two in the afternoon and she was still wearing pajamas. She could not remember the last time she'd done something like this. "Circumstances," she said under her breath, as she pulled on jeans and a sweatshirt.

"All done," Jaxon yelled as she was putting on her sneakers.

"Okay, sweetie, Mama will be right there." She didn't really believe Jaxon could have finished his sandwich so quickly but obviously he was anxious to go play. There were usually kids his age at the park this time of day and even if there weren't, he still liked playing in the sand pit with his trucks. It was so cute how he moved dirt around with a miniature earthmover and then tried to make buildings out of sticks and leaves and whatever else he could find. She started to laugh as she thought about it and then her breath seemed to catch in her throat. "Earthmovers," she said out loud, as a picture of Gray's new golf resort formed in her head. In her mind's eye she could see the huge earthmovers off in the distance as construction crews busied themselves with the building. She visibly shivered as she realized that there was more to this father-son connection than just Jaxon's looks.

It was a beautiful day and once they were at the park, Cassidy's mind eased a little. As she sat on a bench near the sand box that Jaxon loved to play in, she could feel her neck and shoulder muscles loosen. She didn't know if it was the sun on her back or the sounds of a distant lawn mower, birds chirping in nearby trees and bees buzzing by, but she felt relaxed, almost as relaxed as she'd been that night, sitting on that beautiful patio in Hawaii, when she'd met Gray.

"Gray Griffin," she whispered and shivered because of the memory. His name alone did things to her system. She couldn't help wondering if she would have spent the evening—and the night—with him if she had known who he really was. She couldn't completely nix the idea that his wealth and reputation might have completely intimidated her, had she'd known the truth. She had always been shy about some things, after all. And that could have been the reason why he had suggested they remain anonymous to each other.

Now that she thought about it, she was sure he had kept his identity hidden because of who he was. It all made sense now, especially his comments about women wanting a marriage proposal before accepting a dinner invitation. He'd probably been with more than one woman who'd dated him because of his wealth. And then, out of the blue, Cassidy's gut wrenched. She was startled to realize her discomfort had been caused by the thought of Gray with another woman.

"Oh, come on," she told herself. "He didn't learn his incredible bedroom moves through osmosis." Of course, he'd been with other women, just as she'd been with other men. That normal fact of life, however, didn't make her gut feel any better. In truth, the more she pictured Gray in the bedroom, *any* bedroom, the more her stomach had to deal with those pesky butterflies.

"Look, Mama," Jaxon said, as he pointed a tiny finger at the road he'd just built. It snaked through the sandbox and he'd even managed to connect the end with the beginning.

"I see, sweetheart," she told him. "You are a very good road builder."

Jaxon began collecting twigs and leaves and placing them beside his road.

"Wha'cha got there, sweetie?" Cassidy asked.

"Houses," Jaxon replied.

He was building an entire neighborhood. Cassidy just shook her head and marveled at her son. He was a brilliant little guy, which she'd recognized many times during his three years of life. Oh, how Gray would adore him! Any father would. But he could not have him, he couldn't! She shrank within the light jacket she'd worn, hiding from something she couldn't clearly identify, but she'd honestly never been more frightened of anything in her life. She sighed heavily and forced her attention to Jaxon's construction project, which made the little boy very happy.

Two hours later they were home and Jaxon was put into the bathtub. He'd somehow gotten sand, dirt and twigs inside his clothes, his hair and on his face, not to mention under his fingernails.

"How did you get so dirty?" Cassidy asked her son, not really expecting an answer.

"The park," he said, rather matter-of-factly. "It's dirty, Mama.

"It certainly is."

Cassidy made a wonderful spaghetti dinner for them and then sent Jaxon to his room to play while she cleaned the kitchen. Just as she finished up, Caroline returned with a plate of home-made peanut butter cookies.

"I guess I know what you and your sister did today," Cassidy said, as she bit into one of the delicious cookies.

"Angela had to bake something for the church potluck this Sunday," Caroline explained. "It was either cake or cookies. We decided to do both."

"And where's the cake?"

Caroline laughed. "If I had brought home both you'd have eaten both and then I'd be in trouble."

"You got that right," Cassidy said, already thinking about having a cookie with her morning coffee.

After reading a story to Jaxon and tucking him into bed, Cassidy went to her office to see if she could get some work done. The only thing she had actually accomplished that day was to get the Fletcher project pushed up to accommodate a wedding party. Not that the project was small potatoes, but she still felt guilty for having spent most of the day playing with her son.

She sat down in front of her computer, switched it on so that she could check her email and began thinking about what she would need to do for work tomorrow. She was in the middle of several projects and now with the new Griffin International project looming on the horizon, she would need to reassign some of the work that she had intended to do herself.

"Griffin International …" she said aloud. She still had not called Gray. She glanced at the clock she had hanging on the wall. It was nearly 8:30 p.m. It had been at least twelve hours since he had called her office. "Why," she again spoke out loud. "What does he want?" There was, of course, only one way to find out. She looked at the clock again. Should she call now, she wondered? It was still fairly early in the evening and she did have his cell number.

Cassidy went to the living room where she'd set her phone down on the coffee table when they had gotten home from the park. As she picked it up, those damned little butterflies returned with a vengeance. She nearly doubled over with all the fluttering that was going on. Instead, she sat on the sofa while she looked at the numbers that Diane had sent her. And for a third time, she sought out a clock and for a third time discovered it was still only eight-thirty.

"He'll be at home by now," she whispered. "But what if he isn't alone?" Cassidy sank into the couch as that thought took hold. He could easily be married or even living with someone and that may have been the reason why he had acted the way he did when they met again in his office. That would make sense. It would also make sense that he simply wasn't interested in anything more than a second-night stand with her. After all, she couldn't doubt that he'd enjoyed their first. She sighed and mumbled, "But why, really, did he call?"

She was driving herself crazy with these off the wall thoughts and knew that she should just pull up her big girl panties and call him. That would be the only way she would ever find out the answers to the questions eating her alive. Or would it?

"David!" she said aloud. She could call him in the morning and explain that she'd been home sick the day before and had just found out that Gray had called. She could tell him that she knew how busy "Mr. Griffin" was, so she called David instead so that she didn't disturb his boss. Surely, he would know the reason for Gray's call, as long as it was business related. And if David had no idea? Then she would know that Gray had called for personal reasons. And that possibility gave her butterflies another jolt.

"Don't count your chickens," she told herself, as she made her way back to her office. At least with a plan, albeit a flimsy one, she would be able to get some work done. "And hopefully get some sleep tonight."

Gray sat staring out of the large picture window of his penthouse condo. A light rain had begun to fall, normal for the area, and there were millions of tiny droplets impairing the magnificent view he had of downtown Seattle. He didn't care, though, as he wasn't really looking at anything in particular. He checked his watch for a final time before retiring for the night.

It was just after eleven and his phone sat silent on the table next to him.

five

*C*assidy woke up feeling fairly refreshed. She'd still had a few odd dreams but nothing that had kept her awake like the night before. After showering, fixing her hair and putting on her makeup she went to the closet and picked out a favorite dress. Wearing this fun Tommy Hilfiger color block dress with a swing skirt always made her feel a little sassy. She paired the short-sleeved dress with a jacket and a pair of high-heeled pumps. She needed to feel good today and once she got a look at herself in the full-length mirror she had in her bedroom, she felt great!

"Wow!" Caroline exclaimed, once she'd entered the kitchen. "You certainly look better than you did yesterday."

"Thank you," Cassidy told her nanny. "I feel better."

"I'd better go get Jaxon up and dressed," Caroline said.

Cassidy nodded as she got her morning coffee. She also grabbed a cookie and sat down at the table to eat it while Caroline got Jaxon ready for his day. She never left the house without her special time with her son. She just couldn't leave without telling him that she loved him and getting a hug from that precious bundle of energy.

Cassidy finished her coffee and put her cup in the dishwasher and went to the couch to wait for the sound of little feet running down the hall. When they didn't come and instead, she heard Caroline in the hall, she knew something was wrong.

"What is it?" Cassidy asked, meeting Caroline where the hall and living room intersected.

"He was a little cranky and felt warm, so I took his temperature," Caroline explained. "He has a mild fever. Just 99.7 but it's making him feel a little bit off."

Cassidy went to Jaxon's room to find her son sitting on the edge of his bed. "Sweetie, what's wrong?" she asked, going to his side and sitting down. "Don't you feel very well?"

"I go with you today," he said.

"Oh, honey, I wish you could, but Mommy has to go to work."

"No, we go to park."

Cassidy picked him up and put him on her lap. "We'll go this weekend, I promise." These were the mornings that she just hated having to work for a living. If only there was a way that she could stay with him all the time, working from home when she wanted and still make enough money to support them both. But working only part-time did not pay the bills. And while her book was considered successful in the interior design business it wasn't like a Nora Roberts best seller.

Jaxon snuggled down and clung to her, burying his face in her breasts. She looked helplessly at Caroline who was standing in the doorway. Caroline came to the bed and tried to take him.

"No!" Jaxon hollered, and grabbed his mother tighter.

"Sweetie, Mommy has to go to work," she said, as soothingly as she could. "Caroline is going to make … French toast for you." Caroline smiled and nodded. That was actually Jaxon's favorite, and seemed to appease him enough for her to pass him to the nanny, though her heart was breaking when she did.

"I just hate leaving when he doesn't feel good," Cassidy said to Caroline. "You do have his medicine, right?"

"I know exactly where it is," Caroline said. "And try not to worry. I'll keep an eye on the fever and let you know if it gets any higher."

Cassidy decided she would work a half day in the office and come home as she had done in the past when Jaxon wasn't feeling well. And that was the thought she held onto as she left the house and drove to work. If she hadn't told herself she would be home soon, she knew she would never be able to leave.

The office was alive with activity as Cassidy entered the building. All three of her designers were in their cubicles, the phones were ringing, and she could hear the light clacking of computer keyboards. As she rounded the corner to her office, Jennifer called out to her.

"Hey, Cassidy, I got the area rugs for Mrs. Fletcher," she said. "They're in the conference room."

"Thanks, Jen," Cassidy said. "I'll take a look at them in a few minutes." Then to Diane, she asked, "Any messages?"

"Good morning to you too," Diane said as she handed her two small, pink papers.

"Sorry," Cassidy said. "Jaxon has a fever, and you know how that always discombobulates me. Good morning."

"Did he get what you had?" Diane asked.

He definitely did not have what she had. "I don't …" she said hesitating. "Caroline is keeping an eye on him, but I'll probably leave early."

"And how are you feeling today?"

"I'm fine," she told her assistant. "I think I was just overly tired. I did get a good night sleep last night though, so we'll see." And the reason she got any sleep at all was because of her plan to call David this morning. "Listen, I need to make a call this morning so please see that I'm not disturbed. I'll open my door when I'm finished."

"Certainly," Diane said, with a smile. "No calls, and no one enters."

Cassidy sat down at her desk, put her purse away and picked up the phone. Taking a deep breath, she dialed up David Wainright.

Gray wasn't sure how he should feel about Cassidy not calling him the day before. He thought about calling her office again and even found his hand moving to the telephone on his desk more than once. He had stopped himself though, because he wasn't sure that this wasn't Cass's way of telling him that she wasn't interested. Of course, there could be a dozen other reasons too. Hadn't her assistant told him that she was working from home yesterday? Maybe Cassidy left instructions that she wasn't to be disturbed unless it was an emergency and if that was the case then maybe she just hadn't gotten the message yet.

A light knock on the door to his office brought his full attention back to work. "Yes?" he called out.

"Sorry to bother you, Gray," David said as he opened his boss's door. "But Cassidy Roark just called and—"

"Cassidy Roark?" Gray asked, interrupting David. "Cassidy called you?"

"Yes, I just got off the phone with her."

Well, this was dammed odd! "What did she want?"

"She said that you telephoned her yesterday and she was returning the call," David tried explaining.

"Then why didn't she actually return the call … to me?" Gray asked with tones of exasperation creeping into his voice.

David knew the man sitting behind his desk all too well and he could tell that Gray was getting angry though over what, he had no idea. "She said that she knew you were busy and didn't want to disturb you. She was just wondering why we had called since there was no other message other than that she needed to call back as soon as possible. I told her that I didn't know why you'd called but I would find out."

Gray felt his blood pressure rising. He had not wanted to let David, or anyone for that matter, know that he'd phoned Cass. This was personal and he'd wanted to keep it that way. But was that any reason for him to get angry with David? It wasn't

David's fault that she'd called him instead. "Look," Gray began after he took a moment to calm himself down. "You know how I like to stay involved and get to know the people that we work with and since I didn't really have a chance to sit down and talk with her when we met, I thought I'd call her and maybe set up an appointment to meet with her one afternoon."

David nodded, accepting what he'd just heard. "Okay, I'll call her back and set something up."

"Why don't you hold off on that," Gray said, knowing that he needed a few minutes at least to digest this latest turn of event. "I've got a call in to … ah … and I may have another meeting. I'll let you know when I'm ready to meet with her again."

"What should I tell her in the meantime?" David asked. "She's expecting me to call her back."

Yeah, well, I was expecting her to call me back too, Gray thought. To David, he said, "Give me till noon to figure out my schedule. It won't hurt her to wait a few hours for a call back."

"Very good," David said. He then turned and left Gray's office.

Gray spun around so that he was facing the windows, put his elbows on the arms of his large leather chair and laced his fingers together with his two index fingers pointing straight up, slowly tapping them together as he thought. What was Cass up to, he wondered? Why wouldn't she call him back directly? Did she believe the agreement they had made in Hawaii was still ruling their lives? But wouldn't she know that he wasn't living by it anymore by his phone call to her? "Maybe not," he said out loud.

His mind drifted back to the morning he had left her lying in bed in her hotel room. She looked so beautiful with her thick, black hair cascading across the pillow and a clean, white sheet barely covering her naked form. If only he could go back in time, he would do that morning completely different. He would make her get up and go to the airport with him, telling her along the way who he really was. Then he would get her pertinent information, address, and phone numbers and as soon as he landed in Spain, he would send his jet back for her.

But would she have agreed to all of that? She did have her own life and obviously she had made a name for herself. She had her own design business and she'd even written a book. Would she have done any of that if he'd whisked her off to Spain to be his … what? Mistress?

Gray stopped tapping his fingers together. What did he want from her? "First things first," he said quietly. And the first thing he needed to do was get to know her better. He needed to find out what she wanted out of life. And he needed to know whether or not she wanted anything to do with him. Her not calling him back could be an indication of her feelings, but if that were the case, he wanted to hear it directly from her lips, no going through David or even using the telephone. He wanted to hear it from her in person.

A plan began forming in his head, a plan to get her alone so that they could talk. But where? Would she meet with him alone if she knew it was him she was meeting? By her response or rather non-response to his phone call yesterday, he doubted that she would. Gray turned around and picked up the phone on his desk and dialed David's number.

"Hi, Gray, what can I do for you?" David said.

"What's going on at the Bainbridge Island project?" This particular hotel was the second that they planned on working on once the golf resort was close to completion.

"Nothing," David said. "I sent your ideas over to the architect last Monday so we're now in waiting mode. Once we get the blueprints, we can …"

"That's fine, David," Gray told his assistant. "I was thinking that this might be a good day to take Cassidy over there. I mean, it's pretty loud and hectic with a lot of construction going on unlike at the golf resort so you could probably get more accomplished without a lot of people around."

"That's true," David agreed. "But is it too soon? She hasn't even had time to work on the first project yet."

"If we wait, then there will be construction there too. Besides, it might be good to bring her into a project so that she can see the entire thing from beginning to end."

"I see your point. I'll call her and see if she's free."

Cassidy had been surprised by David's call. She half expected that after he'd spoken to Gray, he would be calling to say that they had selected another design team. Instead, he wanted to meet her on Bainbridge Island to see another project. And what had Gray wanted? David was very vague about that. He said something about his boss wanting to get to know her better and would set up an appointment with her at a later date.

After checking with Caroline to make sure that Jaxon was okay, Cassidy had arranged to meet David at the new project at 2:30 p.m. She had Diane look up the schedule for the Bainbridge Island Ferry. She would take her car on the Ferry with her so that she could easily get around. And while she'd traveled to the island before, it had been only twice, and she hadn't actually noticed how people got around. She had gone with friends and they had walked everywhere.

Diane came to her office door. "The Ferry takes about 35 minutes, give or take, so you should probably take the 1:10 p.m. That will still give you plenty of time to find the resort."

"David gave me directions so hopefully I won't get lost!"

"The good thing is that it's an island," Diane chided. "You can only go so far in any direction before you run into water."

Cassidy spent the rest of her morning going through her current projects and reassigning them. This would lessen her load so that she could concentrate more on Griffin International. She also selected the designer that would assist on this account. Jennifer had been next in line for a project of this size so she had been delighted to tell the designer that she would be assisting her. She also wanted to take her this afternoon to meet David.

"How about a trip to Bainbridge Island this afternoon? You can meet our contact and see the new project first-hand." she asked Jennifer, once they discussed the Griffin projects.

"Oh, I'd love to go!" Jennifer exclaimed. "When do we leave?"

"We'll be catching the 1:10 p.m. ferry."

"Perfect … oh … what about Mrs. Fletcher's rugs?" Jennifer asked, referring to the project that Cassidy had managed to move up the day before. "The painting will be done by noon today and they're going to start delivering furniture tomorrow. Shouldn't the rugs go down before the furniture arrives?"

"You're right," Cassidy said. "Darn, I really wanted you to meet David. Oh well, I guess we'll have to schedule a lunch with him next week. After the lunch with him, we'll take a drive over to the golf resort."

"Sounds good," Jennifer said. "Have you looked at the rugs I got at the Seattle Market yet?"

"Nope, let's take a look now."

So far, Gray's plan was working. Cassidy had agreed to go to Bainbridge Island to meet with David. Now all he had to do was make sure that David was too busy to go so that he could take the young man's place.

Gray leafed through a few files to see what he could give David to do and came upon the perfect thing. David had been asking for more responsibility with regards to selecting and working on his own projects within the Griffin International family. David felt that after six years under Gray's tutelage he knew what types of ventures Gray was interested in. Gray picked up the phone and made an appointment with a realtor in Coeur D'Alene, Idaho, for the next morning. Then he called David into his office.

"You've been asking to go out alone and look at potential property for Griffin International," Gray began, once David had entered and sat down. He then slid a manila file folder across his desk. "Go take a look at this land for me. It's in Coeur D'Alene, Idaho, and I've already made an appointment for you for tomorrow morning. You'll have to leave this afternoon and spend the night there but that will give you a chance to look the area over before your meeting tomorrow. If it looks good, we'll go back together in a few days and make the deal. I'll rely totally on your judgment, if you think you're up to it."

David was so excited that he nearly forgot about his appointment with Cassidy. "Thank you, Gray. This is … thank you! I'll finish up what's on my desk and then I'll … oh … what about Cassidy Roark? I'm supposed to meet with her this afternoon. Should I cancel or postpone?"

"That's right," Gray said trying to sound as if he had only just remembered. "I completely forgot about that when I made your appointment in Coeur d'Alene. I guess we could postpone your trip a few days."

David looked dejected. "Yes, sir, we could. But if the land is really good another buyer may come along."

Gray had a hard time stifling a laugh. "That's true," he managed to say. "Maybe you should go ahead and go. I'd hate to miss out."

"But, what about Cassidy?"

"Well, I guess I could go in your place," Gray offered. "That will give me some time to get to know her."

"That's right!" David said excitedly. "You did want to spend some time with her. But, what about your other appointment? You said you were waiting for a call back from … someone."

"Oh, right, he called back and said he can't meet until next week."

Gray almost felt bad for what he'd done—almost. The thought of seeing Cass alone quelled any discomforting thoughts of his bad deeds. He checked his watch and saw that it was nearly 10:30 a.m. He'd wanted to make sure that he was on the island well before her, so there wouldn't be any chance of her seeing him before she arrived. He picked up his cell phone and headed for the parking garage.

It was a beautiful day and Cassidy was excited to be getting out. The only thing that would make this trip better was if Jaxon were with her. He would love riding on the ferry, and he would really love that they could drive onto it. She made a mental note to make sure a trip to Bainbridge with Jaxon was in the not-too-distant future.

Once she and her vehicle were safely aboard, she pulled out her phone and called home. Caroline had told her that Jaxon was doing great and his fever was back to normal but with children, it was hard to tell when they were actually coming down with a bug. They simply didn't know how to tell you that they weren't feeling up to par.

"How's he doing?" Cassidy asked, as soon as Caroline picked up.

"Right as rain," Caroline answered. "If you saw him now, you'd swear that we were just imagining things this morning."

"I'm glad to hear that," Cassidy said. "But I'm still a little concerned. That fever didn't come out of nowhere."

"I'm keeping tabs on his temperature, Cassidy. I take it once an hour so if anything comes up, I'll let you know right away."

"Thanks, Caroline." Once again, she thanked her lucky stars for finding this woman.

The ride to the island took exactly thirty-five minutes, just as Diane had said, but it was an enjoyable half hour. Cassidy was expecting to see David on the ferry and was very surprised when she didn't. She thought about calling him but then decided that he'd taken the 12:25 p.m. instead of the 1:10 p.m. Maybe he had a favorite restaurant on the island and wanted to have lunch before their meeting? Or perhaps he had other things to attend to like making the place safe for her arrival.

David's directions were terrific and within 20 minutes she was pulling into the entrance of the Bainbridge Island Resort. According to David, this was going to be a spa and wellness center. They were going to build European mud baths, a fitness complex and have nutritionists and doctors on staff. This resort was going to rebuild a person's mind and body through massage, relaxation, fitness, and nutrition. Cassidy wondered where one could sign up for this extraordinary experience.

"Hmmm, no David," she said, noticing that hers was the only car parked out front. Maybe he was still at lunch? "Or maybe he missed the ferry," she said out loud. "That would explain why I didn't see him." She checked her phone for missed calls but saw none. She decided she would call him if he didn't show up in a few minutes or so. In the meantime, she would get out of her car and take some pictures.

Her digital camera was small and fit easily in her jacket pocket. She left her purse in her car so that she wouldn't have to worry about setting it down in the dirt while she took photos of the outside of the building and the grounds. She began with the front of the building and snapped a few shots of the entrance before she noticed that a small rock had been placed to keep the front door open just an inch or two. David was here, he'd just parked somewhere else. There was probably a back entrance where employees had parked when this resort had been open. She opened the door and stuck her head inside.

"Hello?" she called out. "David?"

When she didn't hear him calling back to her, she stepped inside. The reception area was fairly small with a check-in desk a few yards back from the front doors. To the left was a couch in a horrid shade of orange and to the right were chairs, same orange upholstery. Off the reception area in either direction were long hallways. She looked right first and saw the manager's office and then a set of stairs and guest rooms. To the left was a huge picture window and door to the outside courtyard and pool area. Beyond that door, more rooms. She took a few steps toward the picture window to get a better view of the pool. That was when she heard something behind her. A shuffle or a stirring of some kind.

Cassidy swung around, hoping what she was hearing was just David stepping into the reception area. It wasn't.

"Hello, Cass."

six

Cassidy's breath caught in her throat at the sight of the tall, sandy-haired man standing across the reception area from her. His hands were stuffed into the pockets of his tailored black pants. The button on his suit coat was done up but because of his stance she could see a small triangle of white shirt between the front panels of the jacket along with a buckle from the black belt around his waist. His head was tilted slightly to the right and his beautiful green eyes were looking directly into hers. If it was at all possible, he was even more handsome than the night she'd met him in Hawaii.

"Hello, Gray," she finally said, feeling her entire body beginning to tremble. Not so much that he would notice, she hoped, and what possible explanation could she come up with should he ask why she was shaking?

"I, ah, I know you were expecting David, but I came because I wanted to apologize to you," he said, shuffling his feet a little. Cassidy had seen Jaxon do this exact same thing when he'd been caught doing something naughty.

"For what?" she asked, truly perplexed about the reason for this meeting.

Gray could see that she was a little unnerved, which disturbed him, so he rushed ahead to try to make her feel better. Still, his voice wasn't as strong as he liked. "My, ah, reaction to seeing you again," he began a little stiffly. "I certainly wasn't expecting you, of all people, to be standing there in my office when I turned around."

She took a breath and wondered what on earth he was getting at. "Sorry to disappoint you," she said flatly, hoping she was handling the situation with at least a little grace.

This was not going at all the way Gray had planned. And hoped for. He took a moment to collect his thoughts and in that moment with the two of them staring into each other's eyes, all he could think about was running across the room, grabbing her up into his arms and kissing her with all of the pent-up passion he'd been forced to live with since they had met and parted. He forced his gaze away from her gorgeous blue eyes and spoke with genuine enthusiasm. "That's not what I meant," he said. He took a half step in her direction and then resumed eye contact. "In fact, quite the opposite is true."

"Go on," Cassidy said, and if she had been trembling a little before, she was now trembling a whole lot.

"Cass, you have no idea how many times I've thought about you over these last—"

"Four years, it's been four years since we met in Hawaii." A fact that was absolutely impossible for her to forget now.

"Four years and one month," he added. "Give me a minute and I'll have the exact number of days as well."

Cassidy felt her trembling subsiding as her heart began to race. Had he kept track too? She smiled. "That won't be necessary."

He shuffled his feet again and managed to move another step closer to her. "Truth be told," he said. "I owe you another apology."

"And what would that be for?" she asked, with renewed puzzlement.

"For leaving you that morning without finding out your last name and getting, at the very least, your phone number," he explained. "I should have had my head examined. People don't find what we shared in that, that … one perfect night very often in life."

Cassidy's heart felt like it might explode with an overload of joy. He still thought it was a perfect night. And then her cheeks grew warm at the thought of their bedroom romp. "It was … ah … I'd like you to know something, Gray, I don't normally do things like that," she said. "I mean, I don't fall into bed with men I've just met."

"I don't either, Cass," he said, moving closer yet. "And I don't know if you will believe this or not, but that was never my intention when I proposed our evening together. All I really wanted from you was a dinner companion and some good conversation. You seemed so fun and playful, especially when you suggested we take the place of the Jensens. I thought you'd be someone I could spend a nice evening with. But then … I don't know … something happened between us … something I considered special."

Cassidy could not hold back a huge smile. It had been special for her as well. But then why hadn't he—

"I must have thought about trying to find you at least a thousand times," he continued.

"What stopped you?" she asked, thinking he was somehow reading her mind.

"Honestly, I don't even know anymore. I thought it was because of the agreement we'd made, at least that's what I told myself. It might have just as easily been my own fears."

"Fears?" Cassidy asked, genuinely surprised. "What were you afraid of?"

"Of us, I think, of the connection we'd made," he told her. "That has never happened to me before, Cass. And then time got away from me and I guess I was afraid to find out that you had completely moved on. I didn't want to know that you were with someone else, so I just buried myself in work."

"Oh, Gray," she said, now taking a step closer to him. "I was silently praying that you would break the agreement and I almost followed you out to the airport to try to find you that morning. I didn't want it to end either."

"Really?"

She smiled one of her dazzling smiles and nodded.

"Maybe we can start over," he offered. "Start fresh."

"How would we do that?" she asked. "I mean, our … history together doesn't leave much for the imagination, does it?"

Gray was now standing less than two feet from her. "Maybe that's a good thing. I mean, we already know we're great in bed together … now we'll have the fun of getting to know each other on a more personal level."

"You can't get much more personal than what we've already done," Cassidy said, with pink cheeks and a laugh.

Gray laughed too. "Yes, but bedroom compatibility is half the battle. Now if we find we like each other's … other attributes, we've got it made."

"So, where do we begin?"

Gray removed his right hand from his pants pocket and held it out to her. "Hi," he said. "My name is Gray Griffin."

She stared deeply into his eyes for a moment and then reached out with her right hand too. "Hi. I'm Cassidy Roark."

As soon as their hands touched, it was like a hot, searing bolt of lightning, right where their palms met, it shot through their singed flesh, like flowing electricity through bare wires. Nothing could have pulled them apart at that moment. It would have been like trying to put a cork in a volcano to try to stop an eruption. And still holding her hand in his, Gray put his left arm around her back and pulled her into him, finding her lips with his and taking them hungrily.

Cassidy felt both dizzy and wild as Gray's lips met hers. This was something she had dreamed about over and over again during the last four years, one month and however many days it had been since their incredible encounter. Yes, she had to admit that she had thought often of Gray's touch and his kisses all over her body. Lordy, how she had wanted to feel him inside of her again. And from what she could feel from the hand he was still holding, now against his body, he wanted that as much as she did.

Gray was so pleased that Cassidy didn't pull away from him, didn't even try to resist his kiss. In fact, she was kissing him back with all the passion and fervor of their first meeting. As their tongues met and played together, he slid his left hand down her back to her bottom and then slowly began lifting her skirt. He wanted, no he needed to feel her female moisture, the soft petals of flesh and the heat they held inside. And when he moved his hand to the front of her panties and slid his fingers inside, she groaned with pleasure.

Was this happening? Was she really here with Gray again, kissing him, feeling his manliness, and wanting? Or was this a dream she would wake up from as she had done so many times before? And then his fingers were touching her most intimate places, caressing and rubbing, probing and stroking. She groaned. She couldn't help it as the things he was doing to her were just too delicious. But this wasn't fair, she thought, he should be receiving the same kind of attention from her. That was when she pulled her hand away from his and then used both to unbuckle his belt, and ever so slowly, unzip his pants, releasing his now fully engorged member. And when she grabbed him with both hands, he groaned too.

"Cass," he said through ragged breaths. "Oh, Cass, I want you like I've never wanted another woman in my life!"

"Then take me," she said, her voice hoarse with desire.

Somehow, they found themselves up against a wall, which wall Cassidy had no idea, but at this point she didn't care. But with his height compared to hers, this position would never work.

Until, that is, he put both hands on her bottom and easily lifted her to the perfect height.

"I'll need your help here," he said huskily.

She smiled as she wrapped her legs around his waist, pulled her panties aside and guided him to the place he needed to be, and then when he thrust himself inside her she thought she might explode. How could anything feel so damn good?

It didn't take long once he was inside of her, feeling her wet heat, for him to reach the pinnacle. He tried to hold off, tried to last a little longer to make sure that she was ready too, but being there, back between her beautiful legs, feeling her soft flesh against his was just too much, he cried out at the release of spasms that rocked his entire body. But was she done? Had he pleased her?

"Cass did you …?" he asked as he set her down.

She smiled. "It's okay, I don't have to …"

But before she could finish her sentence, he was on his knees in front of her. First, he completely removed her panties so that he would have full access. Then, he began suckling and licking her exactly where he knew she liked it. And when her breath caught in her throat and her body tightened, he knew he'd done his job.

"Gray!" she called, as her knees turned to rubber.

They found themselves sitting on the floor in the hallway with his arm around her shoulders and her leaning against his chest. "This carpet is really disgusting," she said, looking around at where they were. "I hope you intend on changing it."

"I think that's your job," he teased.

She looked up at him with raised eyebrows. "So, did I pass the interview? Did I get the job?"

He bent over and kissed her softly on the lips. "I think you already know the answer to that."

After taking a few minutes to get themselves together, Gray walked Cassidy to her car. "Can we have dinner tonight?" he asked, while opening the door of her SUV.

She smiled dreamily. She would like nothing more than to sit across a table from this man tonight. "I think that would be …" But she couldn't, could she? Didn't she have something else she should be doing? After all, she had a life, a home … and a son.

"So, it's a yes?" he asked.

"Ah … I think … can I get a rain check?" she asked, pulling herself back into reality.

He just looked at her.

"I mean, I wasn't expecting … this when I came out here today and … I have plans already." That wasn't really a lie, was it?

"Oh, sure," he said. "I guess this was a surprise for both of us. How about this weekend?"

Weekends were reserved for Jaxon, no exceptions. "How about next Monday or Tuesday night?"

"You have plans for the weekend too?"

She shrugged. "Like I said …"

"Okay, then give me your address and I'll pick you up Monday night."

Oh Lord, she could not let him come to her house. Not yet anyway. "Can we meet?"

"Meet?" he questioned.

"Yes, I could come to your office and we could go from there?"

"I guess so."

"It's just that, well, I'm really busy at work right now, you see, I've got this demanding new client … and I've been putting in extra hours so that I can sort things out enough to fully concentrate on just him." She was trying to phrase it so that he would think she was working harder so that she could spend more time with him and his business. "It would be easier for me to go to you. You don't really mind, do you?"

"No," he told her, realizing that he didn't care how or when he saw her again, just as long as he did. "I don't mind. So, can we say it's a date then? Monday night we'll meet at my office at seven o'clock?"

She nodded. "Are you coming back on the ferry with me?"

"I have a few things to do here yet," he told her. "I'm not sure I'll make it, so I'll probably catch the next one. But before I forget, what's your phone number?"

Cassidy slid behind the wheel of her vehicle and reached into her purse for a slip of paper and a pen. When she did, she noticed her cell phone which she had left on the seat next to her purse and saw that she had a missed call. She quickly swiped the face of her phone and saw that it had been Caroline. Jaxon, she thought, it had to be about Jaxon. She quickly wrote down her number and handed it to Gray. And as soon as he took it, she started the car's engine and said, "I'll see you Monday." And then just as quickly, she shut the door, put her car in drive and pulled away, giving him nothing more than a little wave as she did.

"What the hell?" he asked aloud as he watched her leaving, seemingly as fast as she could.

Cassidy knew not to try to drive and look at her cell phone at the same time, but she wasn't far from the port. And just as soon as she was in line to drive onto the ferry, she engaged the Bluetooth and dialed her home number. Something had to be wrong with her son; Caroline never called just to chat.

"Caroline, it's me," she said, once her nanny picked up. "What's wrong?"

"Nothing serious," Caroline told her. "Jaxon's nose started to run about an hour ago and his fever came back. I gave him some medicine and now we're on the couch together watching one of his movies. His fever is down again but that poor little nose is all stuffed up. Do you want to talk to him?"

"Yes, please put him on."

Cassidy could hear Caroline tell Jaxon that his mother was on the line and then she heard that little stuffed up voice, "Hi Mama."

"Sweetheart," she said. "How are you feeling?"

"Okay, we watch pea-pan." That was how he pronounced Peter Pan.

"Good for you," she said, feeling terribly guilty that she wasn't there and even worse that she hadn't been available to answer Caroline's call. "Mama will be home soon. Now, please give the phone back to, Caroline."

"It's going to take me about an hour to get home," Cassidy told her once she was back on the line.

"Don't rush," Caroline said. "I'm keeping him quiet and for now, he's fine."

It was time for Cassidy to drive onto the Ferry. "Okay, I've got to go, but I am on my way." And once she was parked and out of her car, twenty shades of guilt engulfed her.

She was supposed to be working, instead, she was with Gray.

She should have had her phone with her instead of leaving it in the car, while she was with Gray.

She should have been available when Caroline called, instead, she was with Gray.

She should have been home with Jaxon, instead, she was with Gray.

And what was she doing with Gray? "Oh, Lord!" she said quietly, as she stood near one of the ferry's railings staring down at the water. How had this happened? How had she allowed this man to seduce her again so easily? But had it really been all his fault? Hardly! She had participated and eagerly at that. And what was worse, she'd almost accepted a dinner invitation from him without a single thought for her responsibilities at home, namely her son. What was it about this man that so enraptured her and caused her to completely lose track of everything else including her commonsense?

Soon, the boat was moving but not nearly fast enough. She wanted nothing more than to put distance between herself and …

"Hello, Cass."

As long as he was there, Gray had been planning on walking the entire resort again, making additional notes and taking some more pictures. He still loved getting personally involved in his projects. He still loved the day-to-day work and planning. He knew that once he no longer found the little things enjoyable, it would be time for him to do something else. But as he entered the front doors of his building again, he could not stop thinking about Cassidy and the way she left. It was almost like she was fleeing a fire.

Gray couldn't help but smile as he thought about the fire they had created just a short time ago, and only a few feet from where he was standing. Maybe that was the fire she was running from? That thought didn't sit well with him.

Instead of doing what he'd intended, Gray turned around and locked the doors. He made his way to the back of the building where he'd parked his car. He slid in behind the wheel and started the engine just as fast as Cassidy had started hers. And within moments, he was on the road to the ferry. He wasn't going to let her get away from him again, at least not like before. She seemed upset over something and if it was because of what they had done today, then he wanted to talk to her about it, in person and as soon as possible.

His was the last car allowed on the ferry for that crossing. He could see Cassidy was near the front of the ship, and he watched as she got out of her car and climbed the stairs to the upper deck. As soon as he could, he followed her up. She was standing near the port side railing and seemed to be staring down at the water. He walked up behind her.

"Hello, Cass," he said, for the second time that day.

seven

Cassidy felt that odd sense of déjà vu when she heard Gray's voice behind her. She also felt a tingling deep down in her nether regions as he spoke her name. My God, she thought, my body reacts to just the sound of his voice. That was the magic he held over her. How on earth would she ever be able to function normally around him when all she wanted to do, with just the sound of his voice in her ear, was rip his clothes off and have her way with him.

"I thought you were taking the next ferry," she said, as she turned around to face him.

"Sorry to disappoint you," he said, taking her line.

"Quite the opposite is true," she said, repeating his words back to him.

He smiled and looked down at the deck and then back up at her. "It felt like something was wrong when you left," he told her. "I didn't want … I don't want there to be any miscommunication between us again, Cass. I want nothing but total honesty from you, and I promise you will get the same from me. That's the only way this will work."

Cassidy swallowed hard. Now would be the time to tell him about Jaxon. You have a son, she wanted to blurt out. He looks exactly like you and now I can see that he acts like you too. Instead, she smiled and nodded. The words simply would not form on her lips and all she could do was wonder why. What was she so afraid of?

"So, why did you leave the way you did?" he asked, when she didn't speak right away.

"I had a call that I needed to return," she said, not lying exactly.

"Was it about the plans you have this evening?" he asked, almost afraid to hear the answer.

"Yes," she answered.

Gray's eyes narrowed. "Cass, are you seeing someone else tonight?"

"It's not what you think, Gray," she tried explaining. "I don't have a boyfriend. In fact, it's been a long time since I've even dated." Since the day she had found out that she was pregnant with Gray's child, there had been no more dating, no more men in her life. And once Jaxon was born, he became the only male she even wanted to spend time with. Until now, that is. But did she dare tell him any of that?

"Then what?" he asked. "What is so important that you can't cancel it and spend the evening with me? It's been a long time,

Cass, and I can't think of anything I'd rather do more tonight than reconnect with you."

Cassidy's heart felt like it was being torn into a million little pieces. She would love to spend the evening and even the entire night with him. And she would love to bring Jaxon along and introduce him to his father. So again, she tried to say it, tried hard to utter those four little words, you have a son. But again, she found herself unable to speak.

Gray could not figure out what had his beautiful Cass so twisted up about. If there wasn't another man in her life, then why was she so upset? He moved closer to her and took her in his arms and found that she was trembling all over. "Cass, what is it?"

She stepped back from him. "Please, Gray, please don't ask me. Let me tell you in my own way," she said. "And I promise, with all my heart, I promise that I will explain everything to you. Just not now, not today."

Gray was so puzzled. On the one hand, she was within arm's reach and obviously willing to *be* with him. On the other hand, she was clearly keeping something from him. "I don't like secrets, Cass," he said. "I don't like keeping them and I don't like one being kept from me."

Cassidy didn't want to lose this man again, but would her telling him about his son chase him away? Would it cause him to turn his back on her and Jaxon? Would he, at some point down the road, decide he wanted to get to know his son? And if he did, then what? If he pushed her away and fell into the arms of another woman, would she be able to stand the thought of her child, her baby being cared for by him and his new wife? And what would she do with all the feelings she still had for him? Oh,

Lordy, she thought, I really need some time to find out how he really feels about me and whether or not he is even interested in having children. Could she make him understand that without destroying what was building between them?

"Gray," she said, stepping forward and taking his hands in hers. "Everything will become clear if you just give me a little time. I know I said this earlier, but I was not expecting to ever see you again. I've built a life for myself and there are just a few things I need to … to adjust, I guess you could say. If you can bear with me and trust me for the next week or so, well, I promise you'll understand."

Gray melted as he looked into her beautiful blue eyes. And with her hands in his, he could feel the tremendous physical draw they had to one another. Was it worth it to break his own rules just this once? Could he allow himself to trust that she wasn't somehow stringing him along? But, for what purpose, he wondered? He finally nodded. "All right," he told her. "But I have to tell you that this goes against my better judgment."

"I understand," she said. And she really did. She knew that in the next week or two, she was going to have to tell Gray about Jaxon or find a way to leave the planet.

The ferry was getting close to the dock on the Seattle side of the bay. The warning bells sounded and everyone else on the boat started for their cars. Gray pulled Cassidy closer to him and wrapped his arms around her. She had stopped trembling at least, so whatever she'd been so concerned about wasn't currently weighing as heavily on her mind.

"Still on for Monday?" he asked, before they broke their embrace.

"Absolutely," she told him.

"Are there any restrictions on me calling you?"

She looked up into his gorgeous eyes. "None whatsoever."

"So, if I call you at three in the morning …?"

"I'll probably yell at you for waking me, but if you don't mind a tongue lashing, go ahead."

"A tongue lashing from you?" he said with raised eyebrows. "I think I'd like that!"

She blushed. "I'll keep that in mind."

"I guess we'd better go downstairs," Gray said, referring to the fact that they would all too soon need to move their cars. But before they did, they kissed deeply and passionately, one last time.

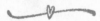

Cassidy called her office as soon as she had driven off the ferry. She needed to check in and let Diane know that she would be going straight home due to Jaxon not feeling well. "Sounds like a cold," she told her assistant. "I'll have to see how he's feeling in the morning; I may be taking him to the doctor tomorrow."

"So, who did you meet with on the island?" Diane asked.

"What do you mean?"

"David Wainright called just after you left and said that he was going out of town, and that Mr. Griffin would probably be there to meet with you," Diane explained. "Was it him, Cassidy, did Gray Griffin, himself, actually show you around the new project?"

Cassidy was certainly glad Diane couldn't see her scorching face. He had done a lot more to her than just show her around the resort. The fact was they hadn't gotten around to seeing anything more than the reception area. She hoped her assistant didn't ask what the property looked like. All she would be able to describe is the dirty carpet. "Ah … yes, it was … Mr. Griffin."

"So, you got to spend some time with him? I heard that he's tall and really, really good looking," Diane continued. "Is that true? And if it is, would you mind introducing me to him? I wouldn't mind going out with a billionaire!"

And that was why Gray had kept his identity from her in Hawaii. Most women reacted just like Diane did to his wealth. "So, just because he has money you would want to go out with him?" Cassidy asked, upset by Diane's remark and trying not to show it.

"No, but having that much money certainly doesn't hurt," Diane said pertly, either ignoring or not hearing irritation in Cassidy's tone.

"I have to go," Cassidy said, knowing full well that if she did not end this call, she was apt to say something to Diane that she would be apologizing for later. And with that, she pushed the end call button on her steering wheel. It was certainly no longer a mystery why Gray had such a hard time meeting women. Good looks and money and not necessarily in that order.

The drive home took forever, as rush hour had just started. She often wondered why they called it rush *hour* when it actually lasted several hours, and no one was moving very quickly. It started at around three-thirty or quarter to four and lasted until well past six o'clock. And if there was some kind of event going on in town then you could forget about getting anywhere on time. If only she could live and work in a less populated area, she lamented. But with her business, she needed to be right in a major metropolitan area to have any success at all.

She sighed as she pulled into her driveway. Why couldn't she just live wherever she wanted and do nothing but write books and take care of her child? Why did life have to be so complicated, she wondered? And speaking of complicated … now on top of everything else she was dealing with in her life, she had one more worry to foul things up, she had to find a way to tell Gray about his son. And she had to do it before he started listening to his *better judgment* again.

Cassidy entered her home and went straight to where Jaxon was lying on the couch with his head on Caroline's lap. They were now watching another Disney favorite of his, Dumbo.

"Hi, Mama," Jaxon said, sitting up as he spoke.

She went and sat down next to him, picking him up and putting him on her lap. "How's Mama's big boy?"

Just then he sneezed, giving her an answer and a good spritzing. Caroline grabbed a couple of tissues off the coffee table and handed them to her. Cassidy wiped his nose and herself. "How's the fever?" she asked Caroline.

"It's still down," Caroline answered. "Now that the cold has come out, I don't think we'll have to worry about fever anymore."

"You're probably right," Cassidy agreed. "Has he eaten much today?"

"A little French toast this morning and half a banana. Lunch was just a little macaroni and cheese. He says he's not hungry."

"Do we have any soup?"

"I don't think so, but I can run down to the store and get some," Caroline offered.

"Would you mind?" Cassidy asked. "If I'd had my thinking cap on, I could have stopped on my way home."

"No problem," Caroline said, as she stood up and went down the hall to get her purse.

Cassidy felt bad. She should have stopped at the store herself, but she had been thinking about other things. She'd, once again, been thinking about Gray. "I'm a terrible mother," she said under her breath. How could she be thinking about a man, any man, rather than her precious son? Of course, she knew she wasn't really a bad mom, but she still felt a ton of guilt over her recent adventure with Gray. And with those thoughts came the tingling sensation she'd felt on the ferry again. How did just thinking of this man make her want him all over again?

"I'll be right back," Caroline said, as she stopped where the hallway met the living room before heading for the front door.

"Thank you," Cassidy said, unable to look at the woman for fear she would be able to read her thoughts and know the way she was feeling from her scarlet cheeks and the deliciously sinful look that had to be in her eyes.

Jaxon had turned around and was back to watching his movie. He seemed fine now and completely oblivious to his nose plight. Cassidy decided to go change out of her work clothes while he was so engrossed with the little elephant on the television screen.

"Mama's going to change her clothes," Cassidy told her son, as she moved him from her lap back to the couch. "You stay here and watch your movie. I'll be back in a minute."

He was so entranced with what he was watching that he didn't even say anything back to her. She just smiled as she got up and started to walk down the hall to her bedroom. About halfway there, her cell phone started to ring. She turned around and went back to the coffee table where she had set her purse down.

"Ta-phone, Mama," Jaxon said.

"That's right, sweetie," she said, as she grabbed the phone out of her purse. And though the number looked familiar, she couldn't immediately identify it. "Hello?" she said into the phone.

"Hey, beautiful."

It was Gray. The mere sound of his voice turned her insides to jelly. "Hey, yourself," she said back to him as she took her phone with her to her bedroom.

"Are you back at work?" he asked.

"Ah, no, actually I'm at home."

"I wish I were there with you," he told her.

"And then I wouldn't get any work done at all," she said, in a teasing vein.

"Nope, I would see to it that you didn't."

"Are you back at work?" she asked, ignoring his sexual inference.

"Yes, I stopped in to make sure the roof wasn't falling in," he chided.

"Somehow I think your people are probably pretty capable."

He laughed. "I see you're getting to know me. Now we just have to work on me getting to know you better."

"Tell me something," Cassidy said. "What ever happened to David? He was the one who called me for today's meeting and then you're the one who showed up. How did you manage that?"

Gray really laughed then. "It wasn't all that difficult."

"So, you did set it all up," Cassidy said.

"I did," Gray admitted. "Cass, I had to speak with you. I had to know if you had any feelings for me whatsoever. And I wanted you to know how I felt about you. You do know, don't you?"

Cassidy bit her bottom lip. She knew that Gray was physically attracted to her, that much was certain. But did she know how he felt about her emotionally? No, not at all. She was about to say something else and then his words from the boat filled her head, I want total honesty from you. "I guess I don't, Gray," she finally said.

The phone line went so silent that Cassidy was ready to believe that they had been disconnected. "Gray, are you there?"

When Gray drove off the ferry, he seriously contemplated following Cassidy. He now knew she had a secret she was keeping from him and for the life of him, he could not figure out what it was. But would following her give him his answer? Probably not. In fact, the only thing following her might do, if she spotted him, was destroy any trust she may have in him. He decided it would be best if he went to his office instead.

But calling her, that was a different story.

Gray entered his building and went straight up to his office where he would have privacy, fully intending to make a call to Cassidy. His secretary, however, had other ideas. He had several phone calls to return and at least three important emails that needed his immediate attention. It took him almost an hour to get through his necessary business before he could do the one thing that he really wanted to do, which was to talk with the raven-haired beauty that had him so captivated.

"Hey, beautiful," he said, once she'd picked up. Evidently, she had been telling the truth about him being able to call whenever he wanted. That made him happy and eased his mind some. Their conversation remained light until he brought up feelings, their feelings for each other.

Now, he had no one to blame but himself for the corner he'd painted himself into and she was waiting for a response. How exactly did he feel about her? He thought she was gorgeous and sexy, and she had a quick wit that he adored. She was obviously smart, her business and her published book were proof of that, and she seemed just as attracted to him as he was to her. Her most important attribute though was that she was so easy to be around, with a gift for the gab that had them both talking like they had known each other for years, when they'd only just met in Hawaii.

And he thought about her nearly all the time. He thought about her when he was drinking his morning coffee. He thought about her when he was driving to the office. He thought about her as he sat behind his big mahogany desk and tried to concentrate on work. Had he fallen in love with her? Maybe it wasn't full-on love yet, but he was definitely heading in that direction. On the other hand …

Gray swallowed back words of love and opted for, "You're very special to me, Cass. I've known that since we met. Like I said before, something happened between us that I can't explain with simple words. I want to explore that, and I hope you do too."

Cassidy didn't know what she was expecting from Gray but for him to say that she was special to him and that he wanted to explore their feelings for each other made her heart skip a beat. "You're special to me too, Gray," she said. "I do think we need more time to get to know each other better ..."

"I'm all for that," he said eagerly.

"You didn't let me finish," she admonished lightly. "I was going to say that we need to know each other better outside the bedroom."

He chuckled. "You're right. But can we still do the bedroom stuff while we're getting to know each other too?"

"Gray, you're incorrigible!"

"All right, let's say that there will be no ... bedroom stuff ... Monday night," he offered. "We'll go out and have a nice dinner somewhere in public and do nothing but talk. Deal?"

"Deal"

Their call ended with a reaffirmation of their plans for Monday night. Once he got off the phone, though, all Gray could think about was that it would be four long days before he saw her again, unless he could figure out a way to see her sooner. It was something to ponder that was for certain.

"Juice, Mama?" Cassidy heard, as she pushed the hang-up button on her phone.

She turned to see her son standing in the doorway to her bedroom. One of his little hands was on the doorjamb and the other held his empty sippy cup. As he looked at her, he tilted his head to the right and started shuffling his feet, all the while his beautiful green eyes stared directly into hers. And at that moment she recognized once again, just since seeing Gray, that her adorable son was an exact miniature of his father. Other than size, their likeness was so clear and defined that she felt an ache in the vicinity of her heart. At least that was the spot she blamed for her angst.

She shook her head and got up off the bed where she had sat down to take the call from Gray. How could she not tell him about his son? How could she ever live with herself if she even attempted to keep them apart? Cassidy had been raised with strong family values and a huge sense of right and wrong. To not tell Gray about Jaxon would go against the grain of her values and would be completely and utterly wrong.

"I've got to find a way to tell him," Cassidy said to herself. "And I've got to do it soon."

eight

Cassidy spent the next several days in absolute joy and utter agony. The joy came from Jaxon and all the little things he did, like climbing onto her lap and hugging her for no apparent reason. And the way he was picking things up and learning something new every single minute of every single day or so it seemed. It amazed her and she loved watching him as he figured out how to do something on his own. She could just see the little wheels turning in his head and knew that she could sit with him for hours on end and never get bored.

There was also joy where Gray was concerned. He called her every day. And he always tried to get her to drop whatever she was doing to go to him. There was some agony there as well. She would have loved to be able to spend time with him, hell she would have loved to spend the entire weekend with him.

But she couldn't. And on the one hand, she didn't mind because she and Jaxon were together as they usually were. And just one week ago, that had been enough for her. The truth was, if Gray had not re-entered her life it still would have been enough. His return, though, made her start thinking of some of the things she was missing in life. She was, after all, still a young, vibrant woman with all the wants and needs of a young, vibrant woman. How had she managed to ignore and even suppress those feelings for four years?

The agony came whenever she allowed herself to think about what telling Gray about his son could mean. And there were so many possibilities. He could turn and run away from them, which would leave them no worse off than they were right now. Life would return to the *normal* she had known since Jaxon was born. She would have to find a way to abolish her feelings for Gray again, but she had done it once, and though a painful prospect, was doable.

Gray could also want to be a part of his son's life. That too could mean so many different things. For one, he could merely want to spend time with the little guy … regardless of his and Cassidy's personal relationship. For another, he could want shared custody and shared responsibility. He could also want the three of them to live as a family. And that was the lovely picture Cassidy clung to even when the last scenario, the scary scenario, the one that could so easily keep her up at night, entered her brain and took seed there. That final possibility, the one in which Gray decided he wanted Jaxon for himself alone, the one that completely excluded her was so terrifying she lost the ability to breathe normally whenever it bombarded her senses.

And while she didn't know why he would ever do such a thing it was still a horrifying possibility.

Saturday had been spent at home baking cookies with Jaxon and that was because he still had the sniffles, but by Sunday he was obviously feeling better, so they ventured out to the park for an hour. It was her evenings that had changed the most, and that was because the evening hours were when Gray called.

Every night around eight-thirty her phone rang. It was almost as if he knew that she put Jaxon to bed at eight and would be free to talk. And talk they did. Saturday night they talked until one in the morning. By the time she got off the phone that night he knew what her favorite food was, her favorite color and her favorite dress designer. Of course, she had found out a few things about him as well. He loved old rock music from the sixties and seventies, he hated oysters and he loved to travel. He'd even said he wanted to take her to some of his favorite places in the South of France. The one thing they did not discuss, the topic she was saving for their next in-person conversation, was the one thing she was almost desperate to hear his feelings for—or against—and that was family.

"Mama!" Jaxon exclaimed, as he ran down the hall Monday morning to greet his mother.

As she swept him up in her arms she turned to Caroline and spoke tentatively. "I will be late getting home tonight."

"Shall I fix dinner for Jaxon?" Caroline asked, taking her employer's announcement in stride as she always did.

"I'm afraid you might have to put him to bed too," Cassidy went on, feeling a little uneasy about laying her own bedtime routine on the nanny. Still, there was no overlooking her plans for the evening, so this was merely a necessary conversation.

She took a breath and continued. "I'm not sure exactly how late I'll be, Caroline, but I have a feeling I won't be home before ten ... or eleven."

Caroline smiled, her expression as calm as always. "Okay," she simply said.

"Dinner with ... a new client," she said, feeling bad about the lie and unsure why she felt compelled to explain. And while Gray was indeed a new client, that was not her reason for having dinner with him. She hoped that her guilty eyes weren't giving away the fact that she was going on a date.

"No problem," Caroline said, with what Cassidy swore was a little smirk on her face, even though any such response would be completely out of character for the woman. Cassidy then decided with some self-disgust that her imagination was running a little wild. It was possibly understandable with so many worrying nerves darting here and there throughout her system, but maybe, just maybe, Caroline had seen the sexy blue dress that was hanging in the hallway next to the front door and had figured out that her employer wasn't exactly telling the truth.

She was letting the situation get her down, Cassidy thought. With a big sigh, she gave Jaxon a goodbye kiss, set him down, grabbed her purse and dress, and left. And her final explanation of that unimportant little scene in her foyer was to recognize once again that Caroline was far from being a stupid woman. Of course, she knew Cassidy had fibbed.

But for pity's sake, why on earth had she lied about her date with Gray? Would Caroline quit her job because her employer was going out on a date? It was too silly to even consider.

She managed to shove that morning's concern to the back burner, but the day seemed to drag. She knew it was because of her upcoming date and the conversation she was planning to have with Gray. She even thought that tonight might be the night she would tell him about Jaxon. If he was receptive to discussion and open about his feelings on the subject of family then there wouldn't be any need for her to keep her son, *their* son, a secret any longer.

At one point during the day, Diane had tried to talk to her about Gray again. She had brought in a magazine and told Cassidy that there was an article about him in it. She'd reiterated that if there was any chance, she would love to meet him. Cassidy tried not to visibly tighten up in front of her assistant. She even thought of telling Diane that she was having dinner with him that very evening but then thought better of it. What if things didn't work out between her and Gray? Did she really want her employees to know that she had even dated him? And what about Jaxon? Right now, no one knew who his father was. It wouldn't be hard to put two and two together if they met Gray in person though, or if Diane really studied the pictures of him in the magazine, and Diane might do exactly that if she knew of Cassidy's date this evening.

As soon as Diane left her office, Cassidy opened the magazine and turned to the article her assistant had referred to. The first page was a full black and white photo of Gray looking directly into the camera. There was absolutely no mistaking whose eyes Jaxon had. Cassidy had to smile as she read the title of the article, *Seattle's Own Billionaire Playboy Extraordinaire*.

Diane stopped in once again, just before leaving for the day. "I can stay on if you need me," Diane said. "I don't have any plans this evening."

"Not necessary," Cassidy said. "I don't plan to be here much longer myself."

"Okay, well, I'm off then," Diane said. "You have a good evening and give that adorable little boy of yours a hug for me."

Cassidy was trying to behave normally; all the while her insides were jumping around like little Mexican jumping beans! "Will do and you have a good evening too."

Finally, she was alone, and the building was quiet. With her stomach in knots and getting worse the closer it got to seven, she got up and strode to the bathroom where she discovered mascara under her eyes, streaks in her eyeshadow and no lipstick left at all. Thank goodness she had time to fix herself up. She would hate showing up at Gray's office looking the way she did now.

By six-thirty, Cassidy, once again, looked fabulous. She had completely redone her makeup and hair and was now standing in front of the bathroom mirror in a cocktail length, Eliza J, teal blue, halter dress with lace and A-line skirt. She felt good, much better than a short time ago, and she felt ready. But ready for what? she wondered nervously as she put her car in drive and pulled out of the parking lot.

It took Cassidy twenty minutes to get to the Griffin building which gave her twenty minutes to rehearse what she was going to say to Gray during dinner. She'd even tried anticipating what he might say in return so that she would be prepared for anything. As she pulled into the parking garage of his building, though, she started second guessing the things he might reply, and then when she entered the lobby and saw him standing there next to the security desk waiting for her, looking like an absolute dream, exactly like that magazine photo, everything she had planned to say fell out of her brain. She knew if she looked back to the floor of the garage, she would find her words just lying there, waiting for her to pick them up and use them, but all she could do was stare at him and drink in his male beauty. There he was, tall, lean, and astonishingly good looking in a tailor-made charcoal-grey sharkskin suit, king of all he surveyed.

Especially of her poor, possibly misguided heart.

Gray had spent most of the Friday and weekend before his and Cassidy's date at work. He had long ago learned that if he concentrated on his work, he could actually push all else out of his head. That is until Cassidy came along. That well-tested formula hadn't worked quite so well where she was concerned, and he too often found her beautiful face creeping in through cracks in his mind whenever there was a small lull in the projects in which he was involved. At one point he'd even found himself completely turned away from his desk and computer, staring off at absolutely nothing, with his mind reliving their most recent encounter on Bainbridge Island.

At one point on Saturday, David had returned from Idaho full of energy and wanting to go over every aspect of the land, town, and lake he had just visited on Gray's behalf. That had taken up a good portion of the afternoon, but right before he'd left Gray's office, he'd turned to ask how the meeting with Cassidy on Thursday had gone. And that brought another round of thoughts and feelings and baffling deliberations. Determined to get something, anything, out of her, he'd called her that night and kept her on the phone until 1:00 a.m.

But with all the talking they did, he still could not figure out what she was hiding from him. Yes, he was positive that she was keeping something from him, though what it could be, totally eluded him. He kept asking himself why she would keep *anything* from him, what in her life was so personal to her alone that she couldn't allow him to share it. It made no sense, especially when he let emotion color his memories of Hawaii and of Bainbridge.

But he could only push so hard for answers and had finally decided to assuage his inquisitive mind and wait until she was ready to tell him her secret, although he knew himself well enough that he wouldn't be able to wait indefinitely. Maybe she would open up during their date.

Gray found it difficult just sitting in his office until seven o'clock that evening, the hour that Cassidy was supposed to arrive. He paced, tried watching the news, he even tried lying on one of the sofas in his office before he finally gave up and started wandering around his building. Before long, he found himself on the first floor, talking with the security guard on duty.

"Mr. Griffin," the man said, nodding in the direction of the door leading to the parking garage.

And when Gray turned, he saw Cassidy approaching the glass door. She was so beautiful as she entered the lobby, that the image she created took his breath away. He smiled broadly as she seemed to glide across the floor to him.

"Hey, beautiful," he said, using his now familiar greeting to her.

"Hey, yourself," she returned.

"Are you ready for dinner?"

She nodded even though she did not feel the least bit hungry. It was funny, she thought, *just an hour ago I could have sworn I was famished.*

Gray guided her out to his car and opened the door for her. She had never ridden in a Maserati before but for all she cared, at that moment she could have been climbing into a covered wagon and still been happy because she was with him.

"I made reservations at the Salt Inn," he told her, as he got into the car. "I hope you're in the mood for seafood."

"Anything is fine," Cassidy said, and anything would have been fine, even a cheeseburger and fries if that had been what he'd suggested. "So, how are their fish tacos?" she asked, referencing the dinner they had shared in Hawaii.

He smiled, remembering their first dinner together with true delight. "I can't say they have fish tacos exactly … but … if that's what you really want, we can always go back to Wailea."

"I'm not sure we have time for that tonight," she teased. "We might not make it back for work in the morning."

"I'd make sure we didn't," he said, and he wasn't kidding around.

Cassidy's pulse picked up speed at the thought of spending another night in Hawaii with Gray. Only this time, maybe he wouldn't jump up in the morning and dash off to the airport. Ah, the thought of lying in his arms, feeling his body next to hers, and taking in his scent … she almost groaned at the thought but was able to stop before she completely embarrassed herself.

It didn't take long for Gray to maneuver through traffic and deliver them safely to their destination. Cassidy had never been to the Salt Inn though she had heard of it. This was supposed to be the latest and greatest in seafood restaurants in the Seattle area. Leave it to Gray to get them the best table in the house overlooking the Puget Sound. And from the time they entered the front doors until the time that they were seated, mere seconds had passed. There was no waiting in the bar or waiting in a line or waiting period where Mr. Gray Griffin was concerned.

The ambience was lovely with low wattage sconces on the walls and glowing candles on every table. Soft music played in the background through concealed speakers, and white linen covered the tables. "It's beautiful," Cassidy murmured, as they were seated.

"Thank you," the maître d' said, as he backed away from the table.

Within moments a waiter appeared. He was dressed in a starched white shirt with black trousers and a long white apron. "Can I get you something from the bar?" he offered.

Gray looked at Cassidy.

"A glass of white wine," she replied, taking advantage of their nearness to delve into the depths of his lustrous green eyes. Such an unusual color, she thought again, recalling the first time she'd had the privilege of viewing his handsome features at close range. That had been in Hawaii, of course. Every- thing truly important in my entire life took place in Hawaii, she added thoughtfully. Except for Jaxon's birth.

"Make that two glasses, of the 2016 Penfolds Reserve Chardonnay," Gray told the waiter.

"Very good, sir," the waiter replied. "Would you like to see a menu now or wait until after the wine is served?"

"After the wine," Gray said.

The waiter nodded and disappeared.

"You look beautiful tonight, Cass," Gray said, the second they were alone.

"Thank you," she returned. "You look beautiful yourself if I may be so bold. And you don't have to take my word for it; all you have to do is look around the room."

"Pardon?" he said with a frown and a sweeping but quick glance around, as she'd instructed.

She couldn't hold back a sharp little laugh. "Gray, every woman in here can't keep their eyes off you."

Gray let out a laugh of pure enjoyment. "You're not really serious."

"I'm not? Well, here comes one now."

And sure enough, a pretty, leggy blonde approached their table. "Gray Griffin!" the woman exclaimed. "I heard you were back in town. How have you been and why haven't you called me?"

Gray stood up, shot Cassidy a pleading look, then turned and gave the newcomer a quick hug. "Hello, Terri," he said. "I'd like you to meet Cassidy Roark."

The woman looked at Cassidy for a moment with a *who cares* look on her face. And then all at once, she seemed to recognize who she was looking at. "Wait, Cassidy Roark, the Interior Decorator? Didn't you write a book, or something?"

Cassidy smiled and nodded.

"So, you're Gray's new designer?" the woman said, with a sly little smile shaping her bright red lips.

"She's my date, Terri," Gray said coolly, obviously informing the woman of Cassidy's true status.

Terri raised one eyebrow and then casually pulled a card out of her purse. "Just in case," she said, placing the card in Gray's hand. And then she was gone.

"Wow," was all Cassidy could say, though her mind was going a mile a minute. Was Terri a friend or an ex who didn't like her current status?

But then Gray did something surprising. He took the card and ripped it into tiny little pieces right in front of Cassidy. And as soon as the waiter returned with their wine and menus, he handed the pieces to the young man and asked him to dispose of them.

"Thank you for that," Cassidy said. She meant it even while wondering if her response was appropriate. Tearing the card to shreds seemed just a little overly dramatic, didn't it?

"Are you figuring it out yet?" Gray asked, appearing to settle deeper into his chair.

"Figuring out what?" Cassidy's pulse took off again. Something was coming from Gray, she felt that he was on the verge of saying something serious and this might be the opening she was looking for. "Tell me, Gray," she said softly. "What should I have figured out by now?"

"How I feel about you."

Her heart had begun to flutter, at least that was how her chest felt. But what he'd just said, "How I feel about you," was not an ordinary statement, those words had meaning. Maybe telling Gray about his son would be easier than she had feared. If he was already suggesting that he was falling for her in a serious way …? Don't count your chickens, she warned herself again. She took a deep breath as she looked into his beautiful eyes.

"You look like you have something on your mind," he said, hoping to prompt her into telling him her secret.

"Do I?" she questioned, wondering if she should look at this close and quite lovely moment as the perfect opportunity to tell him about Jaxon. Her abdomen cramped at the thought and she could feel her palms getting sweaty. This decision was life-changing and labeling the opportunity as perfect could very well be going too far out on the limb. She could only tell him about Jaxon once, and if she blurted it out prematurely, she could never take it back. Maybe she should stick to her plan.

She made up her mind and stated in, she hoped, a warm and pleasant way, "Actually, I was just wondering about your family. You haven't said a word about family. You must have some, everyone does."

She had definitely surprised Gray and he wondered why she'd chosen this topic for discussion on what he'd hoped would be a strictly romantic evening together. Regardless, he had to answer. "There's not much to say," he began. "I lost my parents when I was nineteen."

"Oh, Gray, I'm so sorry," Cassidy said, reaching across the table and taking his hand. She had not intended on making him remember painful losses, which the deaths of parents were, no question about it. She'd lost her parents a few years back, which brought tears to her eyes whenever she thought about it.

Gray felt her compassion and shaped a small smile. He put his other hand over the top of hers and squeezed lightly. "It was a long time ago," he told her. "I still miss them, but I don't let it get me down anymore. They wouldn't have wanted me to wallow in grief."

"I'm sure you're right about that. My parents would have felt the same, I'm certain. But what about brothers or sisters?"

"I was an only child." He grinned then. "I am an only child."

Cassidy returned his smile, but she wasn't through asking about family. "Aunts, uncles, grandparents?"

"My grandparents have all passed and my mother's sister is in an adult care facility in Florida," he explained. "I used to go visit my aunt all the time, but she doesn't recognize me anymore. When my visits started upsetting her, the facility asked me to stop coming. They said it took hours to get her calmed down after I left. They said she sometimes mistook me for my father and couldn't understand why I wouldn't bring her sister to see her. Other times she thought I was there to kidnap or harm her in some way."

"That is so sad," Cassidy said, her expression as downcast as her words. "So, you don't have any family at all?"

Gray shook his head.

"Do you want a family?" she asked, thinking the time had finally come for the discussion she really wanted to have with him. If he said yes, then the rest of what she wanted to say would be fairly simple.

Gray's forehead creased with a frown and he cleared his throat before answering, "Do you mean, like a wife and children of my own?"

"Yes," she said with a lovely warm smile. "Like that."

Gray turned his head and looked out at the Puget Sound. "I'm not sure, Cass," he said contemplatively. "I guess I just haven't thought about it much. Besides, my work hasn't left me much time for a wife, let alone children."

Cassidy was sadly startled by Gray's statement. If his work didn't allow time for a family, then why was he always saying things to make her believe otherwise? Was he just playing around with her? Was this a big game to him? She didn't know what to think. He had seemed so intent on getting to know her better ... or had she misread the situation completely? She decided to push the issue a little farther.

"So, all you're interested in is ... what ... friendships?"

Gray turned back to her. "I have friends—"

"Like Terri?" Cassidy interrupted, continuing to push. "Would you consider her a friend?"

"Terri and I used to ... see each other," Gray said slowly, uneasy at this turn but unaware of how to avoid it. "But I think you've already guessed that."

"How long were you seeing her for?" Cassidy knew her question was out of line, but she could not stop herself from asking it.

"I don't know," he said. "I saw her off and on for a few months, I guess."

Cassidy pulled her hand away as she started to wonder why she was even there. The change of subject in their conversation had completely altered her mood. Now she wasn't thinking of Gray's family, or lack thereof, she was thinking of herself. Herself and Jaxon actually, as her son would always take first place in her decisions. But now everything was awry, not just her mood but her emotions, as well. Was this dinner date nothing more than a seduction to him? At the end of their meal would he suggest they go to his place for a night cap even though he had promised it would be strictly dinner and conversation? Or would he say something like how quiet his place would be which would allow them privacy for talking?

"What about serious relationships, Gray?" she asked, with a direct look into the bottomless green eyes she had been admiring only a short time ago. "Have you ever been in love?"

"No," Gray admitted, thinking that honesty was always the best policy. "I don't think so."

"Because you're too busy with work?" she asked, stunned at the speed in which he'd answered what she considered to be a very serious question. "Or because you have no interest in having a wife and children?"

Now it was Gray's turn to be startled. What was Cassidy getting at? "I ah …" He wasn't entirely sure how to answer her. And that was mostly because he had no idea why she was asking questions of this nature. He also wasn't sure how he felt about what she was asking. As he'd just told her a minute ago, he hadn't thought about marriage and kids that much. And maybe that was because he had never met anyone who had prompted such serious thoughts. Until now.

"Are you ready to order?" the waiter asked, seeming to appear out of nowhere.

"Sorry, I haven't even looked at the menu," Cassidy said, with all the calmness she could muster even though she felt a knot of anxiety in the pit of her stomach.

"Give us a few more minutes," Gray told the waiter, without taking his eyes off Cassidy. She had picked up her menu and was seemingly studying it now. "What's the matter, Cass?" he quietly asked, once the waiter left.

"What do you mean, Gray?" she asked, not looking up from the list of dinner options printed in front of her, but not really seeing any of them.

"Come on, Cass," he said. "Let's not start playing games. Was meeting Terri that upsetting to you? You had to know that you weren't my first and I'm sure I wasn't yours. But all that's in the past. We can't dwell on things we can't change."

And there it is, Cassidy thought. Gray will never change, he doesn't want change. He's used to being a bachelor with *friends*. A wife and a child are things, possibly distractions that he's just too busy for. As for her? Was she just another amusing distraction, like Terri had been? So, what would Jaxon be? Maybe another pleasant distraction, but for how long? Would Gray get tired of having a child around as quickly as he did one of his *friends*? Or would he get tired of a child sooner? Children could be trying, any loving parent knew that. Well, she could not, would not do that to her son. She would not introduce him to a father that could someday find him a bother.

Cassidy wanted to be home with her beautiful boy, holding him, reading him a story, and tucking him into bed. That was her life, that was who she was now, and she liked it. As for Gray, she wasn't sure she even wanted to see him again. Billionaire Playboy Extraordinaire? Probably, but that certainly was not what she was looking for in a man.

"You know, Gray," she said finally, setting down her menu. "I'd like to leave."

"You don't like it here?" he asked, totally taken aback. What the hell? he wondered.

"The place is fine, lovely, in fact," she said. "But I want … no, I need to go home." And with that, she picked up her purse and got to her feet.

Gray stood up too. "Just tell me what's wrong." He heard the plea in his voice and wasn't embarrassed by it, either. But what had brought this on?

"What's wrong is that I'm here, and right now this isn't where I want to be," she told him. "Please take me back to my car."

Gray pulled a money clip out of his front pants pocket and dropped two one-hundred-dollar bills on the table. He figured their dinner would have been at least that much and then he turned and followed her to the door. "I wish I knew what's going on with you," he said, annoyance obvious in the tone of his voice.

Cassidy didn't say a word until they were in his car and heading back to the Griffin building. "I'm sorry I spoiled your evening," she told him, able to speak calmly because she had made up her mind about Jaxon's father. Gray Griffin, Seattle's famous Romeo, did not deserve his son and he would never have him. Her next words contained a bit of cynicism. "It's still early, Gray, I'm sure you can find something else to do."

"I didn't want to do anything else, Cassidy," he said. "I was looking forward to tonight since the minute you agreed to go out with me, and I don't understand what happened to change the good mood you were in during our drive to the Inn."

She turned her head and looked out the side window. How could she explain to him that she didn't want to be just another one of his *friends*? She had feelings for him, and she'd had them since Hawaii. And when she'd given birth to his son, she had wished that she knew where he was so she could tell him and share her joy with him. But he wasn't interested in any of that. Clearly, he wasn't above a good romp in the hay with her, but co-parenting? That didn't seem to be a likely prospect at all, not after this evening's conversation.

Once they'd pulled into the parking garage where Cassidy's car was parked, Gray tried one more time. "Cass, if I said or did something, I wish you'd tell me. If this is about Terri, I assure you that it's completely over with her. It's been over for a long time."

Cassidy finally turned and looked at him. He was so handsome and sexy, and she would love to have her way with him one more time. But she knew that would only make matters worse. "I'm sure it is," she finally said, putting her hand on the door handle. "Look, Gray, Hawaii was … it was beautiful and special, and I will always remember it that way. But this is the real world, real life where real people's feelings are at stake …"

"I know that, Cass …"

"Please let me finish, Gray, let me get this out," she said. "My life, my world and yours are so unbelievably different. The things I value and the way I live, I can't just jet off to Hawaii or the South of France like you can. I have responsibilities and I like having them. I have no complaints, no regrets about anything, not even Hawaii. But I just can't, I don't know, live in your world and I won't ask you to try to live in mine. That wouldn't be fair to either of us. I think it's best if we both realize that and go back to where we both belong."

"Are you saying you don't want to see me again?" Gray asked, totally flabbergasted by her little speech.

Cassidy took a deep breath and stated one of the most difficult things she had ever said. "Yes, Gray, that's exactly what I'm saying."

~nine~

light rain had begun falling as Cassidy wheeled her car onto the freeway for her drive home from her date with Gray. She did not want to think about him anymore but couldn't stop their final words from repeating again and again in her head.

After Gray had pulled into the parking garage and parked only a space away from her vehicle, she had told him that she didn't want to see him anymore. "Cassidy, this isn't making any sense!" he had told her before she'd gotten out of his car. "How can you just throw this away?"

"Throw what away, Gray?" she had asked with her very heart in her throat, all but choking her. Yet, she'd continued as this was so critically important. One word from him, the right word, would change everything, her downcast mood, and her plans for the future, every facet of her life. "We don't have anything to throw away! We had one perfect night together in Hawaii and a few minutes of excitement a few days ago. And while I readily admit that we are sexually compatible, I need more than that."

When Gray had just sat and stared at her without another word, she had gotten out of his car and into her own. And without looking back, she'd started her engine and pulled out of the garage. And he didn't try to stop her. Obviously, he wasn't interested in pursuing a serious relationship.

Cassidy checked the clock on the display screen in her car. It was a few minutes after eight. Caroline would be putting Jaxon to bed right now. She used the button on her steering wheel and called home. And after just two rings, Caroline picked up.

"Hello?" Caroline said.

"Caroline, it's me," Cassidy began. "Can you do me a huge favor and keep Jaxon up for a little while longer. I'm on my way home and I'd like to read to him tonight."

"Certainly," Caroline said. "He was asking for you a few minutes ago anyway so I'm sure he'll be glad when you get here."

Cassidy's heart melted and she felt a little choked up. "Thank you, Caroline." Now this is what life is all about, she thought as she disconnected her call.

Gray sat in the parking garage of his building for a good fifteen minutes after Cassidy left. He'd watched her leave and had even thought about trying to stop her so that they could talk this out. But since he really had no idea what had happened and why her attitude had changed so drastically, he'd just sat there and now he was staring at the empty space where her car had been.

What had changed, he wondered for the umpteenth time?

And then a thought occurred to him that made him wince. Maybe she was like all the rest of the women he met. Maybe after she found out who he really was she could not stop herself from wanting a piece of his fortune. And after the things she had said, insistently interrogating him about his family and whether he wanted one of his own, and then saying that she wanted more from him, that painful theory made sense.

He started his car and threw it into reverse. As soon as he was backed out of the spot he had been parked in, he shifted into first and stomped on the gas, his tires squealing as he pulled out of the garage. Damn her anyway! Why did something so good have to end this way? Well, this was one night he wasn't going to spend alone, he decided. Surely Terri would still be at the Salt Inn and he would bet anything that she would be more than willing to see him again.

Upon arriving home, Cassidy had quickly changed into sweats and a t-shirt before going into Jaxon's room. He was in the middle of a big yawn when she opened his door.

"Look who's here," Caroline said. She had obviously been sitting with the little guy trying to keep him awake for his mother.

"Mama!" Jaxon said.

Cassidy's heart melted. How could anything sound sweeter than that little voice calling her Mama? She moved to his bed and quickly took Caroline's place next to him. Caroline padded quietly out of the room and Cassidy picked up Jaxon's favorite book. He snuggled down next to her with his arm lovingly flung over her, and before she had even finished reading the first page, he was sound asleep. He was obviously happy and content, but then so was she. She stayed with him another twenty minutes just watching him sleep and marveled at how fortunate she was to have him.

Once Cassidy left Jaxon's room, she realized that she had not eaten anything since noon and found herself going up the hall to the kitchen. She knew she had ingredients in the fridge to make a sandwich, but what she found when she entered the room was Caroline sitting at the table with a sandwich already made and a tall glass of milk.

"I figured you hadn't eaten," Caroline said, pushing the plate in her direction.

Cassidy was so pleased at this simple kindness that her voice sounded choked up as she uttered a heartfelt, "Thank you."

"You are very welcome. I'm going to turn in," Caroline said. "See you in the morning."

Cassidy nodded. How did Caroline know she hadn't eaten? Was her disastrous date written all over her face? It probably was, she thought dismally as she took her first bite. Obviously, her earlier assessment of Caroline not being a stupid person had just been reaffirmed.

After devouring her food, Cassidy attempted to do a little work on her book. It was still early, only 9:30 p.m. But try as she might to keep her mind on the computer screen in front of her, all she could think of was Gray. His gorgeous eyes looking at her, his beautiful mouth as he spoke her name or kissed her, the adorable way he tilted his head to the right and did nothing more than look at her, oh, how was she ever going to get that man out of her head.

She sighed and exited out of her word program and checked her work email one last time. Once she'd logged in to her email, the first email was from David Wainright. "Oh, no," she said quietly as she opened the email. David wanted to set up a meeting with her to go over her first impression of the Bainbridge Island project. He also wrote that if she had completed any sketches for the golf resort, he would like to see them as well.

Cassidy sat and stared at the email for a full five minutes. She knew what she had to do and that was to compose a letter to him and Griffin International declining the offer to decorate their resorts. She knew she wouldn't be able to do this job even if she was working only with David. Anytime he requested another meeting with her at the Griffin building there was the chance she would run into Gray. And anytime David requested a meeting at a job location, she would not be able to trust that David would be there and not Gray.

Cassidy reopened her word program. This had to be done and it had to be done right away. She wasn't sure yet what she would tell her staff, but she knew she would come up with something. Anything would be better than them all finding out what had happened between her and Gray, and as she had thought earlier, all anyone had to do was look at Jaxon, and then meet Gray, to know that he was his father. This was definitely the right thing to do, even though it would be terribly difficult. She began to type.

Gray re-entered the Salt Inn and went straight to the bar. He ordered a scotch straight up and as he waited for his drink, he scanned the room. Sitting with two other women was the leggy blondee he'd talked to earlier when he was with Cassidy. And when she saw him at the bar, she got up and walked the short distance to where he was standing.

"So, where's your date?" Terri asked, as she took the seat next to Gray, who was still standing.

Gray grabbed his drink and threw it back in one gulp. "I have no idea," he said, as he signaled to the bartender to bring another.

"Did she leave?" Terri asked.

Gray nodded. "Have you seen my new car?" He knew Terri was someone who enjoyed money a little too much, and she would be duly impressed. Cassidy hadn't seemed the least bit impressed ... or was she just better than Terri at hiding her greed for expensive things?

"Haven't seen it, haven't heard about it." Terri said, and then showed him a big smile. "Not yet anyway. What did you get this time?"

"A Maserati," he told her. "I think you'd like it." He immediately saw the glint in Terri's eyes.

"I'm sure I would," Terri said slowly, her voice as seductively sounding as her words.

"Would you like to see it?" Gray asked, as he threw back his second scotch.

"Just give me a minute to grab my sweater and tell my friends I'm leaving," she said.

While she was gone, Gray ordered a third drink. Terri returned just in time to see him slam it down as well. "Ah, I hope you don't think I'm getting in your car with you behind the wheel," she told him.

He reached into his pocket, pulled out his keys and handed them to her. "Not a problem," he said. He then ordered one more drink. "For the road," he told her.

Five minutes later, Terri was sitting in the driver's seat of Gray's gorgeous car with him sitting next to her in the passenger seat. "Where to?" she asked.

"Surprise me," he told her.

"Mmmm … how about your place?" she asked almost coyly.

Gray had to smile. Terri was anything but coy. "Sure," he said. "Why not?"

"Do you still live in the same building or did you buy a bigger, better penthouse somewhere?"

"Same place," Gray said, wondering why Terri would ask if he'd moved into something bigger and better. He didn't upgrade his life that often, did he? Sure, there was a new car every year and he did see his tailor every four to six months. Something about this thought process began to bother him, why was he always trying to change things about his life, why was he always trying to make improvements in the wonderful things he already had? As soon as the woman next whooped as she pulled out of the parking lot of the Salt Inn, though, those thoughts were driven from his mind.

Terri had fun driving his car and took the longer way to downtown Seattle where he lived. Before long though, she was pulling into his personal space in the parking garage of the high rise that housed his condo. "A girl could get used to driving that elegant animal," she said, as they walked to elevators.

Gray put his arm around her shoulders and laughed. Subtlety was not one of Terri's strong suits but at least he knew where he stood with her, unlike Cassidy.

When they entered his condo, Gray went directly to the bar. Terri on the other hand went to the middle of the living room and spun around. He had an almost 360-degree view of the city. "I had forgotten how big and lovely this place is," she said. And Gray's home was truly magnificent. It was two stories of unmatched luxury from the solid wood floors to the floor-to-ceiling windows, surrounding the huge living room. The bathrooms held the finest Italian marble and the bedrooms were decorated with rich Dupioni silks.

"What would you like to drink?" Gray asked his guest.

Terri walked to the bar where Gray was throwing back another scotch. "Hey, slow down there, cowboy," she told him. "You won't be any good to me tonight if you keep that up."

Gray thought about that for a moment. Here was an attractive woman who actually wanted him regardless of the reason. He smiled at her and raised his hand to brush a stray strand of hair from her face. As he stared into her eyes though, her dark brown irises turned light blue. And the blonde hair in his fingers seemed to be darkening to black before his very eyes. He took a step back. "What the …?"

"What's the matter, Gray?"

But that wasn't Terri's voice he was hearing … it was Cassidy's. He shook his head and turned away.

Terri walked around the side of the bar and stepped in front of him, wrapping her arms around his midsection as she did. "You feel so good," she whispered. "I've missed this ... all of this."

Gray needed to fill his head with something other than Cassidy, so he put his arms around her too and pulled her into him, molding her body to fit his. She was taller than Cassidy and thinner, almost bony. "What have you missed?" he asked, trying to ignore the fact that she was not the woman he wanted in his arms.

"I've missed being with you, Gray," she began. "Being seen in public with you is like being seen with Brad Pitt or Tom Cruise. Everyone knows who you are. And forget about waiting for a table, hell the maître 'd's in all the best restaurants in town practically fall all over themselves trying to accommodate you. Do you think I didn't see how fast you were seated tonight with that woman?"

"Is that all you've missed?" he asked. "Good service?"

"No, I've missed this too." She then kissed him on the lips. Softly at first and then she tried to make it more intimate, more passionate." But as she parted her lips, Gray pulled away.

"What's the matter?" she asked, with a big-eyed startled expression.

Gray looked into her eyes again, and again they seemed to turn color. He closed his eyes and Terri took that as a sign that he was ready for another kiss. But as soon as her lips touched his, he pulled away.

Terri dropped her arms and took a step back and it was easy to do because Gray had already lowered his arms. "I'm getting a really strange vibe here, Gray," she said. "Tell me something, why am I here?"

"I'm sorry, Terri," Gray said. "I thought … I guess I just didn't want to be alone tonight."

"Why are you alone tonight? What really happened with your date?"

Gray went around to the other side of the bar and sat on one of the stools. "I … I don't know. All of sudden she wanted to leave, she wanted to go home."

"And she didn't tell you why?"

Gray shook his head. "No, she didn't, and I have no idea what happened. One minute we're having what I thought was a really nice time and the next, she wants to leave."

"Well, whenever I want to go home before a date is technically over, it's because I have someone waiting there for me," Terri offered.

"She's not seeing anyone," Gray said. "Whenever I've called her, she always picks up and we've talked sometimes for hours. It's not another man."

"I didn't necessarily mean another man, Gray," Terri told him. "What about a sick parent or some other relative?"

Gray shrugged. "I guess it could be something like that." He hadn't thought about that, but didn't Cassidy mention that her parents had passed away? But what about aunts or uncles? She had asked him about family, but he hadn't asked about hers. He didn't even know if she had a brother or sister. He frowned at the thought of his own shortcomings when it came to getting to know her better. Maybe that was what had upset her so much. Maybe she had interpreted their time together to be nothing more than him being mildly interested in dinner together, then the necessary foreplay to get her back into his bed. And hadn't she said in Hawaii that it seemed to her like the only thing men were interested in was getting her into bed?

Gray raised his hands and rubbed his temples while groaning out a painful sounding, "Oh, damn!"

"What is it?" Terri asked. "What's wrong?"

"I may have just figured something out," Gray told her. "Hey, would you mind calling it a night?"

Terri sighed. "I kinda figured that we were heading in that direction."

"I'm sorry," he said, as she came around the bar again. He stood up and gave her a hug. "I really am sorry."

"I know," she told him. "Can you call me a cab?"

"I'll drive you," he offered.

"Not after all you've had to drink tonight. Just call a cab."

Gray nodded. "You're right, of course." He then dug into his pocket. "At least let me pay for your ride."

Gray handed Terri some cash and then called for a taxi. As she headed out the door a short time later, she turned back to him to say, "You know, you've really got it bad."

"Pardon?" he asked, not sure what she meant by her statement, or maybe he hadn't heard her correctly.

"Cassidy Roark," she said, almost sharply. "You've really got it bad for her."

Gray sent her a weak grin, but her final remark had teeth, and once she was gone, he thought and thought about it. Did he have it *bad* for Cassidy? In one way he couldn't deny it, for he'd felt smitten at their first meeting. And he was not thinking of their Seattle meeting, their second one. Hawaii had been the most magical event of his life and he had been a fool to pretend otherwise. He might be a lot of things, he was the first to admit, but not a fool. Or he hadn't been while growing up and becoming the man he was today. Hell, he thought, maybe he could no longer judge himself correctly.

He wandered around the condo and started turning off lights as he thought about himself and thought about Cassidy. Why did she have to be so … so … perfect? And maybe she wasn't perfect, but she was perfect for him.

Gray climbed the stairs to his bedroom. It was still early, only about ten o'clock, but he felt more tired than he had ever been. He would get a good night's sleep, and in the morning, refreshed, he would think about Cassidy again and what he should do next. She'd said in plain English that she didn't want to see him again, but there was no way in heaven or hell that he could ever allow himself to believe that it was truly over for them, not yet anyway!

Cassidy had composed what she thought was a very professional letter terminating her relationship with Griffin International. She just hadn't had the nerve to send it yet. She knew it would stir up a hornet's nest of questions, not only from David, but her staff as well, and since she had no idea how she was going to explain it to Diane and the group, she refrained from sending it at all. Instead, she sent it to her work's email address, and as soon as she'd told her employees what she was doing and *why*, she would send it off to David.

She had no clear vision of how Gray would take the news either, but she was sure that he would not be as surprised as everyone else. In fact, he would probably be glad that he wouldn't have to be the one who ended their working relationship.

As soon as she was done with her letter, Cassidy turned off her computer and the lights in her office, and proceeded to walk around her house turning off the other lights that were still burning. She was surprised when she passed by a clock in the kitchen and saw that she'd been working on the letter for over an hour. No wonder it was perfect, at least grammatically, she thought with a little smile.

When she went back through the living room, she stopped at the coffee table and picked up her cell phone. This was a habit she'd had since her father's illness six years ago. During that troubled period of her life, she knew that she would be getting an urgent call and wanted her phone right by her side so that her mother could reach her any time of the day or night. As it turned out, her father had recovered from that illness, but then passed shortly after her mother did the following year. She wished she had her loving parents around her now, especially her mother, so that she could tell her about Gray and ask her advice on what to do.

The house was dark as she padded down the hall to her own room. Across the hall from the master suite was Caroline's room and Cassidy could see by the light under her door that she was still awake. She knew that her nanny was an avid reader, so it didn't surprise her. What did surprise her was when Caroline stuck her head out into the hall and said, "I just wanted to let you know that I'm here if you ever need someone to talk to."

Cassidy smiled. "Thank you, Caroline," she said. "I'm fine, though. Really."

Caroline nodded and pulled her head back into her room. No, thought Cassidy, this woman was definitely not stupid.

Once Cassidy had gotten into her nightshirt and slipped in between the sheets of her comfortable bed she felt relaxed, she felt the stress of the evening melting away like an ice cube on a hot sidewalk. She was at home with her beautiful son sound asleep across the hall. Maybe her house wasn't a mansion or a villa in the South of France, but it was all hers. And she could afford it, as well as a nanny and a good, reliable vehicle. Content, she thought to herself, that's what I am, content.

And her business would survive just fine without the Griffin International account. She'd been doing well so far, with her business growing each year. Maybe not as fast as it would if she kept the huge account, but she had been doing just fine without Gray Griffin.

"Gray," she whispered as her mind drifted back to the day at Bainbridge Island. He had seemed so … what was the word she was looking for? Sincere? He'd seemed so sincere in his desire to start over and to spend time with her, getting to know her. But as soon as he had gotten close enough to touch her again, he was all over her like white on rice.

But that wasn't entirely Gray's fault, she had to admit. She could have stopped him, she could have told him to keep his hands and other parts of his body to himself. She hadn't though, and the reason she hadn't was because she wanted him with as much lust and passion as he wanted her.

So, was their relationship purely physical for both of them?

When she thought about it, it hadn't started out that way in Hawaii. In fact, they'd had a perfectly lovely evening. It had ended in the bedroom but again, that was as much her doing as his. So, what would have happened tonight if she had not pressed him into a conversation that he obviously wasn't ready to have? Would he have simply taken her back to her SUV and kissed her goodnight? And then what? Would they have started dating like normal people? Would he have eventually asked her to live happily ever after with him?

Cassidy's stomach turned over. The night had been going well until she had brought up family. But she'd had a good reason for doing that, hadn't she? She did have a son to think about and Gray was his father. Didn't she have a right to know how he felt about such crucial matters? And now he might never know about Jaxon, which was sad, but he couldn't have it both ways. He was either in or out, not hanging by his thumbs somewhere in between being a lover or a father.

Of course, it meant the same for her. She was turning her back on the most fabulous, most sexually exciting man she had ever met, and she could either continue their affair as it was, or remember that she was a mother first, a woman in love second. That conclusion evoked a huge sigh of self-pity, but it did not alter her determination. Jaxon came first and that was the end of it.

But deep down she knew there would never be an end to the misery she had caused herself. For one thing, she doubted she would ever fall in love with another man, now that Gray had reappeared in her life, kissing her so passionately, culminating in lovemaking so incomparably exciting and fulfilling. In other words, she would live out the remainder of her life without love. At least, a *lover's* kind of love. She would, God willing, have her son and be grateful for that. As for Gray, he might marry some day and have children without ever knowing about his first born. It broke Cassidy's heart to visualize his loss.

It was then that she remembered what he had told her in Hawaii about women wanting a proposal of marriage before even going out with him. And that was exactly the way she'd acted tonight. She had even told him that she wanted more from him. Of course, he didn't say anything when she'd gotten out of his car. He was probably glad to be rid of another gold-digger.

"Oh, Lordy," she said, with a groan of pure misery, "I've really messed this up."

ten

assidy had only been at work fifteen minutes on Tuesday morning, when her cell phone rang. It was Caroline, and since her nanny never called unless something was wrong, she'd grabbed it immediately even though she had two of her designers in her office discussing a project.

"Give me a minute," she said, just before hitting the green button on her cell. "Hi, Caroline, what's wrong?"

"Jaxon's fever has returned," Caroline said. "It's not high, just about a hundred but I thought you should know."

"Can you call his pediatrician and make an appointment for this afternoon?" she asked Caroline. "And then please text me the time and I'll come and take him myself."

"Are you sure?" Caroline asked. "I can take him if you're busy."

157

"Nope, I want to," Cassidy said. "I'd like to talk to the doctor myself. This is the second time in under a week that he's had a fever and I'd like to hear what he has to say about it."

Twenty minutes later, just as Cassidy was finishing up her meeting, Caroline texted her the time of Jaxon's appointment. The only time he could see him today was 12:45 p.m. The doctor would cut his lunch short to see him, but that was the best he could do at such short notice.

"A mother's job is never done," Cassidy said under her breath, as she collected her purse and a few things she would work on from home that afternoon. But before she left the building, she stopped at Diane's desk and asked her to call David Wainright. "He emailed me last night and I haven't had the chance to get back to him yet," she explained to her assistant. "Just tell him I'm still planning on emailing him this afternoon when I get home."

"Sure thing," Diane said. "I'll call him now."

Cassidy was glad she had great people like Diane, not to mention the rest of her crew. They were all hard workers and sincere, every last one of them. And if she didn't have such a wonderful team, she'd never be able to leave like she did whenever it was necessary to take care of her son. It was going to be awfully difficult to tell them that she'd decided not to take on the Griffin projects.

She frowned as she got into her car and started the engine. She should have done it first thing this morning. She should have gathered everyone around as soon as she had arrived and told them what her decision was, no explanation necessary. She was, after all, the boss, the one in charge and the decision maker, period. She should not have to explain the ins and outs of every choice she made when it came to *her* business.

The truth of the matter was that these people weren't just employees, they were all like her extended family now. And they had all done things for her that proved it. Like the time Diane had canceled a date and come over to watch Jaxon when he was just a baby because she and Caroline had both come down with the stomach flu. There was also the time that Bernice, one of her bookkeepers, had spent every evening for a week making party decorations for Jaxon's second birthday. Jennifer had gone with her and Jaxon to the coast one weekend, because she wasn't comfortable with Cassidy and her toddler taking the trip alone.

She could go on and on, she had a similar story with everyone there. However painful it might be, her staff deserved an explanation, and what they really deserved was to hear the truth. But could she do that? Could she stand before them and relate how she had gotten pregnant after having a one-night stand in Hawaii with one of the wealthiest men in the country? Cassidy sighed at the thought of spilling the whole story now. It would undoubtedly open a can of worms that would need explaining, like how did she not know who Gray really was? or how does the big man feel about being presented with a three-year-old son he'd known nothing about? Those were only two of the questions that would cause her current comfortable life to vanish, if everyone who knew her also knew of her sexual misstep four years ago.

Cassidy's stomach turned over as she pulled into her driveway. She'd been picturing herself standing up at a supposed business meeting in her office and announcing to everyone that she had something important to tell them about Jaxon ... and

Gray Griffin. Just putting the two names together made her poor stomach roil in a sickish way.

"I need more time," she groaned, realizing that she had really gotten herself into a pickle this time.

If only she could go back in time, she thought with utter anguish, which was the same fantasy she'd had on and off since Hawaii. And again, she came to the exact same conclusion she'd reached every time: she would do nothing different, if it meant she wouldn't have Jaxon now.

Gray hadn't slept well even though he'd anesthetized himself with alcohol. He simply could not stop thinking about Cassidy and asking himself, or some unknown entity, again and again what could possibly have caused her to behave so strangely. Terri had said the only reason she would ever cut a date short was to meet someone else at home, another guy, obviously, who was waiting there for her. It didn't make sense, though, when he exchanged Cassidy for Terri in that scenario. The two women were so far apart in personality, attitudes, and goals that he felt disloyal for even contemplating Cassidy's participation in something so underhand. Besides, was it even possible for her to have another man in her life when his private investigator had checked her out? Maybe it was possible, he had to admit, but his investigator didn't usually make that kind of error. The man did not just dot all the I's and cross all the T's, he scratched them away and found what was underneath them.

That still didn't make any sense though because when Cassidy had arrived at his office, all dressed up and beautiful, she had seemed happy and ready to go out and be seen in public with him. Then he recalled that she hadn't wanted him picking her up at her home. The memory rushed from the back of his mind to the forefront, knitting his brows together in a deep frown. Why didn't she want him at her house? And why had she told him that she had other plans for the weekend, then spent hours on the phone with him every one of those weekend evenings? Obviously, her plans hadn't included evening activities, so why had she refused seeing him for any after dark dates? Was a big fat deliberate lie the answer to that gnawing question? Damn, did he know her at all?

Gray leaned back in his office chair and shut his eyes. He was downright sleepy, and he considered stretching out on one of his sofas and taking a nap. But even if his body rested, he knew full well that his mind would not shut down.

"Gray?"

Gray opened his eyes to find David standing on the other side of his desk. He must have dozed off even though he had believed sleep was impossible. "Sorry," he said, sitting up straight. "What is it?"

"Well, I was looking over the plans again for the Bainbridge Island project so I could start scheduling some of the demolition, and was wondering what Cassidy thought about your idea to add a gourmet restaurant and lounge overlooking the bay. When you and I talked we discussed adding a high rise to that side of the property with the restaurant on the top floor. That would all take more time, so I could start demolition on that end of the existing building if that's what you two decided."

Once David mentioned Bainbridge Island, the rest of what he said entered Gray's head like gibberish. All he could think about was Cassidy, kissing her, feeling himself inside her, tasting her. He pictured the soft curves of her breasts heaving inside her dress as she grew excited by his touch. And there was no denying her excitement. She had been so wet and ready when he'd entered her that he could barely control his own body. In fact, he hadn't been able to hold out very long but was more than willing to satisfy her with his tongue. He turned away from David so that his assistant would not be able to see his face flushing with want and desire.

"I … ah … we just looked around a little," Gray managed to say, almost normally. "She, ah, had to leave …"

"Was it her kid again?" David asked.

Gray swung around quickly. "Her … what?"

"Doesn't look too serious," Doctor Phillips told Cassidy, as he looked inside Jaxon's ears and down his throat. "A little sinus infection probably brought on by that cold you said he had last week." He stood upright and turned to the worried mother. "I'll give him a dose of antibiotics today and I'll get a prescription for you to give him at home. He'll be fine. Just keep him in the house for the next few days."

"That will be like torture for him," Cassidy said, taking a step closer to her son and putting her arm around him. "He loves going to the park."

"Go to park?" Jaxon said, right before he sneezed.

"See what I mean?" she said to the doctor. "Not today, sweetie," she told Jaxon. "But maybe we'll stop and get some ice cream."

"Yeah, ice keem!"

The doctor smiled and ruffled the boy's sandy-colored hair. "Where did you get that blonde hair, kiddo?" Dr. Philips turned to Cassidy, "I'll be right back." He then left the small room.

Cassidy looked down at her son. She knew exactly where he had gotten that hair from. And that was the question that was going to come for the rest of his life, where had he gotten his light hair, his green eyes, and incredible good looks. She sighed, and not just because other people were going to ask, but soon, he would too. And it wouldn't be long before people in her inner circle, especially Diane, figured it out now that Gray was featured in that Seattle-based magazine.

"Get down?" Jaxon asked.

"In just a minute, sweetie," she told him. "The doctor is going to come with something to make you feel better."

The doctor gave Jaxon a small cup of liquid antibiotics and handed Cassidy a paper prescription. "You should see a difference in a day or two," Dr. Philips told her.

"Will you be wanting to see him again?" Cassidy asked.

"Not necessary," he said. "Unless his fever worsens, which I don't believe it will."

"Thank you, Dr. Philips," Cassidy said. "Come on, sweetie," she said as she lifted Jaxon down from the exam table. "Let's go get you that ice cream."

Before long, Cassidy was pulling into her own driveway. As she did, she looked into the rearview mirror and saw Jaxon's little face covered in chocolate ice cream. She laughed out loud, absolutely delighted with the scene of a very happy and very messy little boy thoroughly enjoying his treat.

"I think you're going to need a bath," she told him, as she pulled him out of his car seat.

"What's the verdict?" Caroline asked, once Cassidy brought Jaxon inside.

"Just a little sinus infection," she told her nanny. "I have medicine for him in my purse."

Caroline took Jaxon from his mother. "I think someone needs a bath," Caroline said.

"That's what I said," Cassidy chimed in. She then pulled the medicine from her purse and handed that to Caroline as well.

"Are you going back to work?" Caroline asked.

"I'm going to work from home this afternoon," Cassidy said. "Just as soon as I get out of this dress and into a pair of sweats."

Caroline smiled. "I'll give him a bath while you get changed."

The two women went their separate ways, Caroline to run a bath for Jaxon and Cassidy to her room to change. Once she was comfortable and in her office, Cassidy called Diane to see what was going on at the office.

"Not much," Diane said, "Oh, I did get hold of David like you asked."

"Oh good," Cassidy said. "And you told him I'll contact him with an email this afternoon?"

"Yep," Diane said. "He seemed a little miffed at first, that it was me and not you calling, but as soon as I told him you were taking your son to the doctor, he got over it fast enough."

"You told him about Jaxon?" Cassidy asked, with her voice rising in tenor.

"I, ah, I did ..." Diane was perplexed by Cassidy's tone change. "I mean, all I said was that you had to take your son to the doctor. Did I say something wrong?"

Cassidy had to stop herself from biting Diane's head off. Why shouldn't she have told the truth? She had never told her assistant or anyone else in the office to say nothing about Jaxon. In fact, most of her clients knew she had a child. Hell, she had told them herself. In this case though, she wished Diane hadn't mentioned him, not to David, Gray's personal assistant. "No, no, I'm sorry, Diane," she said. "I just ... it's just that ... really, it's nothing. I'm just being, you know, a worrywart."

Then she remembered she'd mentioned calling her nanny the first time she'd met David. Of course, it might not have registered with him and Gray hadn't said anything about knowing she had a child. Now she really felt bad.

"What are you worried about?"

Cassidy had to think fast. "Well, you know how some people are, they hear you have a sick child, and they might think you won't be able to handle their job." Well, that was weak, she thought to herself.

"Right," Diane said, sounding only slightly convinced. "I didn't think of it that way. I'll be more careful in the future."

"No, Diane, you're fine, really," Cassidy said, backpedaling as fast as she could. "I'm the one who's sorry. I think ..." And then a thought occurred to her, maybe a way to get out of this whole mess. "... I think I'm a little overworked, overstressed. I may have taken on a little too much right now. It's this Griffin project. I almost feel like I'm running in circles. I'm not sure

taking it on right now was such a good idea. Maybe I should … I don't know … turn it down."

Gray did not trust his own ears at that moment. Had David actually said what he thought he'd heard? Cassidy Roark, his Cassidy, was a mother?

"Her kid," David repeated. "A son."

"How do you know this?"

"Her assistant called me."

"Why?"

"I emailed Cassidy last night before I left the office," David explained. "I guess she didn't have time to get back to me before she had to leave so Diane, her assistant, called to tell me that Cassidy is planning on emailing me when she gets home from taking her son to the doctor. And then I remembered that the day I brought her here to meet you she said something about calling her nanny. Is there something wrong, Gray? Does it matter if she has a child? I'm assuming she must have a husband too. You don't get a kid without a man being involved some-where along the way."

"No, she isn't married," Gray said, without thinking.

"How do you know that?" David asked.

"I guess I'm just assuming," Gray said, a little more thought-fully. "I didn't see a wedding ring when we met last week."

"Now that you mention it," David said. "I haven't noticed her wearing a ring either. Maybe she's divorced."

"Yes, I guess so," Gray said. "Anyway, in answer to your question, I haven't made the final decision on the restaurant and lounge yet. Go ahead and hold off demolition until next week."

"Will do." David turned and headed for the door. Just before he stepped through it, he turned back. "Either she's divorced, or she just never married the guy."

Gray was deep in thought about Cassidy and her child now, so he was a little perplexed by David's last remark. "What are you saying?"

"Cassidy. She's either divorced, or she just never married the father of her child." Then he was gone.

Gray sat and stared at the closed door of his office, thinking about David's final comment. Was Roark a married name? She had never mentioned that it was, but then, he hadn't asked. Why would he? And if it wasn't a married name, then she'd had a child out of wedlock. And so, what if she had? That was her private business and there certainly wasn't anything wrong with that. It was strange though that she had never mentioned her kid in Hawaii. Or was it? He was the one who had set the rules, no personal information.

So, Cassidy had a son. That made perfect sense now that he thought about it. That was probably the reason she was asking him about family and if he ever wanted one of his own. And the boy was most likely the reason she'd had *plans* over the weekend. Maybe he played soccer or baseball and that was why she couldn't date during the day. That still did not explain why she refused to go out to dinner with him at night though. There were plenty of good caregivers in Seattle. And what about the nanny David just mentioned? Surely Cass wouldn't have to stay home every evening with him. Unless …

"Unless he's not very old," Gray said out loud. And if that was the case, then she'd had him after Hawaii.

Gray's mouth went dry as he once again thought about how much time had passed since he and Cassidy had met in Hawaii. As he did, he reached for the telephone on his desk and dialed the number for Paul Radley, P.I.

"Hello, Gray," Paul said, "What can I do for you?"

"Hi, Paul, listen, I asked you to get some information last week on a Cassidy Roark," Gray began.

"Yes, I remember," Paul said.

"I just found out she has a child, and I was wondering …" Gray hesitated for moment. Shouldn't he be talking to Cassidy about this? So far, though she had not even mentioned having a kid. And why was that? Why was she hiding her son from him? If he was just a baby or toddler then she might be concerned that he wouldn't want to be bothered with another man's off-spring. She might even be embarrassed for having a child on her own though she would have no reason to be. But if he was a little older, then … "I'd like to know exactly how old he is."

"Just give me a minute," Paul said. "I have that information right here."

Gray heard tapping like Paul was typing into a computer.

"Yes, here it is," he told Gray. "Her son is almost three and half years old, and his name is Jaxon with an X instead of a ck."

Gray's breath left his body at an alarming rate. So, she was just pregnant when she was in Hawaii, she had gotten pregnant within a week or so of getting home or … she had gotten pregnant the night they had been together. "Can you find a birth certificate for the child?" Gray asked, barely able to get the words out.

"It'll take an hour, maybe less," Paul said. "But, yes, I'm sure I can."

"Do it."

"There's my big guy," Cassidy said, when Jaxon came running into her office after his bath. She picked him up and set him on her lap. Caroline had put him in a pair of clean pajamas instead of getting him redressed. He was so soft and warm and cuddly that Cassidy could not help but nuzzle him and kiss his neck.

"I type?" he asked as he inched his little fingers closer to her computer keyboard.

"No, sweetie, that's Mama's work."

"I work?" he tried again. He loved playing on the computer.

"Not today," she told him. "How about you go to the living room and play with your dinosaurs."

"Okay." He jumped down off her lap and ran into the living room, and then across the carpet to the corner where a toy box was stashed. The location of Cassidy's desk in her office enabled her to watch Jaxon in the other room, and she smiled as he began digging through the toy box, pulling things out that Cassidy assumed were plastic dinosaurs. She turned back to her work which was making a list of all the projects she and her staff were currently working on. She had told Diane a few minutes ago that she felt overworked, so much so that she wasn't sure she should really take on Griffin International as a client. Now she had to prove it. And thirty minutes later, she had quite a list.

"Once everyone sees this, they shouldn't wonder why I'm turning down Griffin," she said, feeling fully justified and emotionally calmer with what she was about to do.

Of course, Diane had made a fairly good point when they'd talked. She had said that Cassidy had been talking about hiring more people a short while ago so maybe now was a good time to do that.

Cassidy sat back in her chair and rolled her eyes. Why did her assistant have to have such a good memory, she wondered? But talking about hiring and being ready to hire were two completely different things. She had first wanted to purchase her building, which having the Griffin account would help her achieve and she'd wanted to remodel the second floor, which having the Griffin account would help her achieve more quickly and … Oh, shut up, she told herself silently.

Cassidy glanced across the living room to where Jaxon was playing. Caroline was sitting on the couch, talking to him and playing. He was showing her things and every so often they would laugh. Cassidy knew she had a lot of work to do, but life was just too damn short. So instead of going to her drafting table where a number of sketches needed completion, she went into the living room and sat down on the floor with her son. It wasn't long before Jaxon was driving tiny cars on her legs and she couldn't have been happier.

"I wonder who that could be?" Caroline said, when the doorbell sounded.

"I'm not expecting anyone," Cassidy said, without any real curiosity. It was probably a salesperson, she thought, not caring enough to get off the floor and find out.

Caroline got up, though, and went to the door. As soon as the nanny opened it, the familiar voice that asked if Cassidy Rourke was available sent a shockwave through Cassidy's system that nearly caused her to lose consciousness.

"Can I tell her whose calling?" Cassidy heard Caroline ask.

Cassidy took a deep breath and marveled that she could breathe at all. "It's okay, Caroline," she said. "Let him come in."

eleven

"You're sure about that?" Gray asked, when Paul Radley called back.

"Yes," Paul said. "There is no father listed on the birth certificate for Cassidy Roark's son."

"What month was he born in?"

"March."

Gray felt the blood drain from his head. He'd met Cassidy in June. Her son had been born exactly nine months later. "What about boyfriends?" Gray asked.

"I can tell you that there's been no one in her life since her son was born," Paul told Gray. "If you want me to go back before that, it will take more time, probably a week or two."

Gray wanted to know a whole lot more but didn't want to wait another week to hear it. It was time for him to do some investigating on his own, even though he knew that doing so would involve Cassidy. He was going to have to confront her, upfront and personal, and though he had no idea how he was going to accomplish it, he wanted to get a look at the child.

"That won't be necessary. Thank you, Paul," Gray said. "Send the bill to my secretary, as usual."

As Gray hung up, he saw his hands were shaking, something he knew he had never seen himself do before. But then, he'd never before discovered that he might be a father. He clasped his hands together in an attempt to calm them. But once separated they began shaking again.

Was this child his? Was he a father? Gray felt as if the room was spinning like a carnival Tilt-A-Whirl, and the only way he was going to get off this ride was to go and see Cassidy and hopefully get a glimpse of her child. But she had made it abundantly clear last night that she did not want to see him anymore, so would she even answer her cell phone if he called? Probably not. Gray picked up his office phone and dialed his secretary.

"Yes, Mr. Griffin?" she said.

"Mrs. Grant, would you please call Cassidy Roark's office for me?" he asked. "Ask for Diane, Ms. Roark's assistant and tell her that we want to messenger something over to Ms. Roark and ask if she will be available this afternoon to receive it." Gray hated being deceitful, but he didn't know any other way to find out where Cassidy was without speaking with her directly. David had said she had taken her son to the doctor, but would she return to her office afterward? If she did, he could go to her office and confront her there. And she would surely have pictures of her child on her desk or walls. Didn't mothers do that?

"Yes, Mr. Griffin," Mrs. Grant said. "I'll do it now."

No more than three minutes passed when Mrs. Grant was calling back. "Ms. Roark is working from home for the rest of the day, but they expect her back in the office first thing in the morning. I told them that we'd send the messenger tomorrow."

"Thank you, Mrs. Grant," Gray said. So, Cassidy was at home … with her child. The only problem now was that he didn't know where *home* was. "Oh, Mrs. Grant," Gray said before hanging up with the woman. "Would you please do me a favor? Would you get the sign-in log from the security desk and bring it to me?"

"Certainly, sir," Mrs. Grant said.

Within minutes Gray had Cassidy's home address in his hand as he made his way down to the parking garage. Everyone who wanted to see him had to sign in with security and had to present picture ID, almost always their driver's license. The guard not only noted the person's name in the log, but he also wrote down their address. After receiving several threats from psychos jealous of his wealth and stature, he had implemented this rule. He'd even hired a personal bodyguard for a while but when the threats amounted to little more than hot air, he'd let the bodyguard go but kept the security rule as a precaution. He was glad now that he had.

Cassidy lived south of the city in an attractive rural community. Gray had always lived in the city believing that the suburbs were for families, soccer moms and dads and the elderly who enjoyed gardening, perfect for those suburbanites but definitely not for him. As he drove through the neighborhood though, he began to alter his opinion. The streets were lined with beautiful houses with manicured lawns, lots of trees and sounds he wasn't sure he'd ever really noticed before. They were comforting sounds of birds chirping, a lawn mower somewhere off in the distance and the wind. He could actually hear the wind blowing through the trees. It was all so pleasant he wondered why he'd been so closed-minded before.

And then he spotted her house. He recognized her SUV, which was parked in the driveway, and as he got closer, he could see the numbers on her house. He was at the right place.

Gray pulled into the driveway behind her vehicle. She was there, inside with a child that was possibly his. His mouth went dry and his hands began to tremble again. Maybe this was a mistake, he thought. Maybe he should just back out of the driveway and … what? Spend the rest of his life wondering if he was the father of Cassidy's son? But if he was, surely, she would have told him. Wouldn't she? She couldn't be that dishonest or cruel, could she?

Then Gray remembered what she had said on the ferry as they rode back to the mainland from Bainbridge Island. When he had told her that he wanted nothing but total honesty from her she'd said that she would tell him everything, just not that day. Was she going to tell him that he had a son? Or was she going to tell him she'd had a child with another man, which actually made more sense. She would probably be afraid that he would not want anything to do with her if she had another man's child and was hoping that he would fall for her before she had to tell him about it. That whole idea was so painful he shoved it away, he needed to stop torturing himself. He needed to knock on that door and find out the truth once and for all.

He swallowed hard and forced himself out of his car. And as he walked up to the front door, he found that he was actually scared. Yet another new experience for him. If this had been another multi-million-dollar deal, he would have been as cool as a cucumber, as they say. But this? He shook his head as he thought about Cassidy having a child in that house. And while there was no denying that fact, he couldn't help but wonder who had fathered the child? Was it him? And that was the question that pushed him forward to the door and propelled his hand to the bell. And though it could not have been more than a few seconds before the door was being opened, it felt like hours.

A woman who wasn't Cassidy opened the door and gave him a quick onceover. Maybe he had the wrong place after all? "Is Cassidy Roark available?" he asked almost tentatively.

"May I tell her whose calling?" the woman asked, still checking him out, he noticed.

Gray was about to tell her when he heard Cassidy's voice coming from somewhere out of sight. "It's okay, Caroline, let him come in."

The woman stepped aside and politely gestured for him to enter. "In here," she told him.

Gray entered the small foyer and as he did, he heard a child's voice. "Look, Mama," the child said. Gray didn't wait for the woman to show him the rest of the way in, he took the few steps across the foyer to the open living area and was stopped dead in his tracks. He did not see the kitchen that was off to his right, he did not observe the hallway that was off to his left, he did not notice the comfortable furnishings, the hardwood floors or the color of the paint that was on the walls. All he saw when he stepped from the foyer into the living room was his own eyes.

Cassidy's mind raced like the speed of light when she heard Gray's voice at her front door. In that split second, she knew exactly what must have happened. David, for whatever reason, had mentioned her child to Gray and he had gotten curious as to why she hadn't told him about Jaxon. And now he was here to find out what was going on. It's time, she told herself, it's time he found out the truth.

"It's okay, Caroline," she called out, amazed at how calm her voice was when her insides were quaking. "Let him come in."

When Gray entered her living room, she watched as the always cool and collected *billionaire playboy* nearly collapsed in front of her. In fact, he had to put his right hand on the wall to steady himself, his eyes never leaving Jaxon. What she had not foreseen was Jaxon's reaction to seeing his father for the first time. When he had heard someone enter their home, a fairly rare occurrence, he'd sat down on her lap and watched as the stranger entered. Usually, he turned away from people he didn't know, and he would bury his face in his mother's chest. This time, he tilted his little head to the right and stared back at Gray.

Cassidy shifted Jaxon from her lap to the floor next to her and then stood up, pulling the boy to his feet. "Caroline, would you please take Jaxon to his room?" she asked.

"Wait," Gray said, his voice cracking but his eyes never leaving Jaxon. "Is he—?"

Cassidy nodded before he finished his sentence.

Gray watched as Caroline walked over, picked up the boy and took him down the hall. He filled his lungs with air and slowly let it out, regaining some of his normal self-control. He then turned his attention to Cassidy who was just standing there watching every move he made. He now had the answer to the question that had bothered him since David had been in his office, he had a son, a little boy that looked exactly like him. But new questions filled his head with the most pressing being, why hadn't she said anything?

Now Gray was staring directly at her. He had finally regained his composure and was standing straight up. He put his hands in his pockets, causing a triangle of white shirt to be outlined by his medium blue suit coat and black belt, just as she'd noticed when she'd seen him on Bainbridge Island. But from the way he was looking at her today, she was certain he wasn't thinking similar thoughts about that meeting. In fact, from the look in his eyes, she knew a storm was brewing.

She took a deep breath. "Gray, I wanted to tell—"

Gray pulled his right hand out of his pocket and held it up in front of her. "Just stop," he told her. He did not want to hear how she'd tried and tried to tell him but had never found the right moment.

"But I'd like to explain—"

"Explain what? All the lies?"

"Gray, I've never lied to you!"

"Not telling me is the same as lying to me," he spat out.

The look on his face made Cassidy's blood run cold. Was that hatred she was seeing? She turned away from him, unable to stand his glare another second. "Maybe you're right," she finally said. "Maybe I should have told you about Jaxon the second I walked into your office and saw you again. But then you acted as though you had absolutely no idea who I was. Do you have any idea how much that hurt? I felt like a tramp just then. I felt like I had been nothing more than a rather insignificant one-night stand."

Gray turned away as well and stared off into her kitchen. Maybe he hadn't handled their *reunion* as well as he could have, but that didn't excuse the fact that once they had seen each other again on Bainbridge, she still hadn't uttered a word about his son. "There were plenty of other times," he said.

"You don't understand," she said, sounding much weaker than she'd like. She had visualized this moment so many times since Jaxon's birth, but none of her hopeful fantasies had delivered such a wallop to her pride and every other female emotion running riot through her system as she was experiencing now. But it was true, she believed wholeheartedly, he didn't understand. Instead, he felt injured, deliberately wounded, and cut off from a truth she should have tripped over her own tongue to express in his office that day, culminating in a speedy and immediate confession, as though she had committed an unpardonable iniquity to his parental rights.

Eventually they turned back to face each other and then stood there for a long moment, just staring at each other, each with their own thoughts. Cassidy's thoughts were focused on why he seemed so intent on blaming her for something that he was as much to blame for.

Gray's thoughts were centered on a question: What was so difficult about doing the right thing? How could she have ever thought she couldn't or shouldn't tell him? He finally opened his mouth. "You're right, I don't understand!" he nearly yelled with so much anger welling up inside him that it frightened him. "I need to get out of here." He turned toward the door.

"Gray, please don't go," she said, thinking that if they didn't talk now, it would only get harder with time. "Let's talk this out. Please!"

He turned back to her. "Now you want to talk?" he questioned. "Last night you couldn't get rid of me fast enough."

"I was just so—"

"Forget it, sweetheart," he growled and within three strides he was out the door.

" … frightened," she whispered, finishing her sentence.

Cassidy was shaking all over and felt so wobbly on her feet that she didn't exactly know how she was going to make it the two steps she had to take to get to the couch. She also felt moisture on her cheeks, lots of moisture.

Caroline appeared out of nowhere. She grabbed Cassidy's arm and helped her to the couch. Then she disappeared but only for a moment. When she returned, she had a damp wash cloth that she placed on Cassidy's forehead. "There, there," she said softly, placing an arm around her employer's shoulders. "Let it out."

Cassidy had not realized until that moment that she was actually sobbing. "I shouldn't have let him in," she wailed. "I should have taken Jaxon and run."

Caroline chuckled sardonically. "That's not the Cassidy I know," she said. "The Cassidy I know is a fighter."

Now it was Cassidy's turn to laugh sardonically. "You have no idea what I'm up against. That man that was just here ..."

" ... Is Gray Griffin, Jaxon's father," Caroline said, finishing Cassidy's sentence.

"How did you know?"

"I've known for about a week now," Caroline explained. "Ever since I picked up the latest issue of Seattle Today. There's quite an article about him in it."

"I know, I saw it," Cassidy said. "How come you didn't say anything?"

"It's not my place," Caroline said. "I was curious though, why I'd never seen him around."

Cassidy sighed. "He didn't know about Jaxon until today."

"You never told him?"

"I would have loved to have been able to tell him," Cassidy said sadly. She then spent the next thirty minutes telling Caroline everything there was to tell about her and Gray, except of course about what they actually did on Bainbridge Island that day. It felt good to finally tell someone the whole story.

"So, he's been out of the country for the last several years?" Caroline asked.

"Yes," Cassidy said with a nod. "From what I understand he's been in Spain. It would not have mattered though even if I had known where he was, I didn't know who he was. I was just starting my business and hadn't yet heard of the great and powerful Gray Griffin. And once I did learn about Griffin International, I didn't know it was the same man. I'd never learned Gray's … my Gray's last name. Oh, Caroline, I know I should have told him so many different times once I had seen him again. I should have told him when I first got to Bainbridge and saw him. I could have easily told him on the ferry back to the mainland. And I definitely should have told him last night. I just chickened out, I guess."

"What had you so concerned?" Caroline asked. "Did you think he'd be a bad father? Did you think your relationship with him wouldn't last if he knew?"

Cassidy thought for a few moments. "I think the thing that terrified me the most was that he might want to take Jaxon away from me."

"But why would he do that? You've provided so well for Jaxon," Caroline said. "You're a good, loving mother, Cassidy. And after I got through testifying, no court in the country would allow that to happen."

Cassidy was so choked up she was barely able to speak. "Thank you, Caroline."

"So, today was the first time he laid eyes on his son?" Caroline asked.

"Yes," Cassidy answered. "And from the way he stormed out of here, it might be the last."

The blood rushing through Gray's veins felt like it was boiling, as he drove almost recklessly out of Cassidy's neighborhood. How could she not tell him? There's not an excuse good enough, he thought as he turned onto the onramp for the freeway heading back into Seattle.

Traffic was heavy the closer he got to downtown and soon it felt like he was crawling. This would never do. He needed to put some distance between himself and Cassidy. What he really needed was the open road so as soon as he came to the off ramp for I-90 East he took that exit. Soon he found himself crossing Mercer Island in the middle of Washington Lake. And before he knew it, he was driving through Issaquah. But it wasn't until he reached the Snoqualmie Pass high up in the mountains that he realized he had no intention of stopping, at least not until he'd put a good, calming distance between himself and Seattle.

Gray used the Bluetooth in his car to call his office. "Mrs. Grant," he told his secretary, once she'd picked up. "I won't be back to the office today, and I might not be back tomorrow either. Please let David know."

"You have an appointment tomorrow morning with Mr. Baxter," she said. "Would you like me to reschedule that?"

Tom Baxter was another developer that he'd occasionally worked with. He'd told Gray that he had something that they might want to pursue together. "No, tell David to take that meeting for me," Gray said. This would be another good opportunity for David to take on more responsibility, as he had been asking to do.

"Very well," Mrs. Grant said.

After hitting the disconnect button on his steering wheel, Gray tuned his satellite radio to a classic rock station and sat back. He hadn't realized he'd been almost perched on his seat, tense and stiff until his back and neck muscles started to ache. Sitting comfortably now and staring at the road in front of him, he started to allow himself to think about Cassidy and what he was going to do about his new situation.

Cassidy had lied to him. Maybe it wasn't an out and out lie, but she hadn't told him about Jaxon. A lie by omission was still a lie, at least in his book it was. The crazy part was that he had known she'd been hiding something, and he had asked her about it. She chose not to tell him. Why? Didn't she want to share her son, their son, with him? And did she still think she wouldn't have to? There were laws in this country to protect a father's rights.

The more Gray thought about those things, the more tense he got. And the more tense he got, the harder he pressed down on the gas pedal. He was doing nearly a hundred before he realized it and slowed down. What he really needed to do was go someplace quiet where he could think, really think about everything and what his next move should be. If nothing else, it would be safer for himself and others on the road today. He certainly didn't want to end up hurting innocent people because he was too distracted to drive in a sensible manner.

Gray shifted his thoughts elsewhere. He turned down the radio and thought about his business. He wished he were back in Spain. The Spanish countryside was beautiful, as was the blue Mediterranean Sea. Not that the Pacific Northwest wasn't lovely with all the tall pine trees and pretty lakes, but Spain was halfway around the world and much more appealing at this moment.

It's funny, he thought, when he was in Spain, he longed to be home. Now he longed to be anywhere but home. That wasn't entirely true, if he was really being honest with himself. He loved Washington State, he loved the sights and sounds of Seattle and he loved all that he had there. The only thing he was not happy with was Cassidy. But that wasn't entirely true either.

When he had first seen her again, he'd been thrilled. He had all but fallen head over heels in love with her when they'd met in Hawaii. And he should have told her so the second he laid eyes on her again. What he should have done was walk around his desk and given her a big hug. But he hadn't. In fact, he'd said nothing. What had she just said that he'd made her feel like, a tramp, an insignificant one-night stand? Nothing could have been further from the truth. He still thought of that night as perfect.

Gray sighed. What he really should have done was ask Paul Radley to find her as soon as he had gotten to Spain. If he had, he would have been with Cassidy when Jaxon was born. Instead, she had given birth to a stranger's child, given him a wonderful home and had also managed to build an impressive business and write a book. And clearly, she was a good mother as she had taken the boy to the doctor herself instead of letting the person, he was assuming was the nanny do it.

Did any of that excuse the fact that she hadn't told him on any of the numerous occasions they'd had together since they had reunited? No, it didn't. But maybe something else did. Maybe looking out for her child excused her. She had been asking him about family at dinner last night. She had asked if he wanted a family of his own. And how had he answered? That his work kept him too busy, Why would she tell him? Why introduce a child to a man who had no interest in pursuing a relationship with a child?

Gray sucked in a deep breath. He was used to making multi-million-dollar deals and keeping his cool every step of the way. When it came to Cass though, he couldn't seem to keep his cool no matter what. Was Terri correct? Did he have it *bad* for her? What else would explain the way he handled this whole situation?

Gray drove another ten miles before he found a place to turn around. It was time he started dealing with his personal life as well as he did his business life. It was time to sit down with Cass and figure this whole thing out, including their child.

twelve

Cassidy and Caroline had spent the hour after Gray left discussing the dilemma that she might now be facing with him, talking about what he might do or try to do, but, in fact, reached no conclusions. How could they? Since they had no idea what the man was thinking or feeling, they had no idea which way he might swing when it came to his son. At one point, Cassidy had suggested that Gray might be out of their lives forever now. In the next breath though, she changed her mind completely.

"This is getting us nowhere fast," Caroline commented. "I think the best thing for you to do is ask him to meet so the two of you can sort it all out."

"I agree," Cassidy finally said, after a long, thoughtful pause. "I'll call him tomorrow and try to set something up."

"Not today?" Caroline questioned.

"You didn't see the way he looked at me when he left," Cassidy said with a shiver. "He was so … so … angry, I guess. And, Caroline, if you had seen his face you might be suggesting I wait to call for another week. Or two." She took a breath and changed the subject though her goosebumps were still in place. "Let's keep this quiet. I'd rather not say anything in front of Jaxon. Not that he would understand …"

"Say no more," Caroline said, returning to her normal calm.

They spent the rest of the afternoon with Jaxon. There was just something in the air that made them both want to spend time with him. And they did not mention Gray's name or talk about him in any way in front of the boy.

Cassidy's nerves gradually settled down, and she had wished Jaxon felt good enough to go to the park, as much for herself as for him. She thought that some fresh air would do her a world of good and even help to clear her mind. But Jaxon's health came before anything else so instead she took him to the kitchen where Caroline was baking sugar cookies. And once the first batch was done, she and her son decorated each cookie with pink, blue and green frosting as well as colorful sprinkles. Once the cookie making and decorating was done, they all went to the living room and watched a movie.

"Again!" Jaxon said, when the movie was done, and the credits began rolling.

Cassidy laughed. "How about you pick out a different movie while Mama fixes supper? Caroline might pull her hair out if she has to watch the same one again."

"I don't mind," Caroline said with a smile. "Whatever he wants." Very often she put Jaxon's wishes ahead of anyone else's, her own included. Her smile was directed at her employer, at Jaxon's mother, and at a woman she now called her friend, and amply displayed the love she had for her little ward.

Cassidy smiled warmly at Caroline knowing exactly how she felt today. "Okay," she said as she hit the play button on the remote to her DVD player. "But remember, you asked for it," she added teasingly. She got up and went to the kitchen to make Chicken Parmesan, one of Jaxon's favorites. He wasn't too thrilled about the broccoli that she made with this dish, but he would always eat a little and a little was better than none.

After dinner was finished and the kitchen was in order again, Cassidy washed Jaxon's hands and face and took him to his room. It was still early, only 7:30 p.m., so she allowed him to play awhile until his bedtime. Caroline went to her room to read and Cassidy sat in the rocking chair to watch her son. He immediately began *building* with his wooden blocks.

Cassidy watched as Jaxon tried to build a structure that was as tall as he was. It fell over several times and he got frustrated. His little brain just couldn't figure out how to make the bottom big enough so it would support the top. "His father could teach him that," Cassidy whispered. "If he was so inclined." Finally, Jaxon gave up on the skyscraper and began using his road grader to clear the blocks and make streets.

About twenty minutes had passed, Jaxon had nearly built an entire neighborhood. He had a street that he had lined with houses and he'd even put in his favorite convenience store on the corner. "I get slushies there," he told his mother.

Just as she laughed, she heard the front doorbell ringing. Jaxon looked at her with big eyes. They never had people stopping by this late. "It's okay, sweetie," she told her son as she stood up. "You finish building and Mama will be back very soon."

As she walked up the hall, her stomach began doing flip-flops. There could only be one person on the other side of that door tonight and she wasn't sure how she felt about that. She turned on the porch light and looked through the peephole on the door. Sure enough, it was him, Gray Griffin.

Gray had raced back to Seattle as fast as he thought he could get away with without endangering others and, yes, himself, since he would not be much good to his son if he didn't make it back alive. And while he drove over the speed limit at times, his Maserati was built for it, he kept it within sensible boundaries.

"My son," he said every so often, trying to digest his own words. "I have a son."

As Gray started closing in on Seattle, he felt like he was racing against time. When he had left Cassidy's house it was a little after 2:00 p.m. It was now 7:30 p.m. and he still had some distance to go. If he ran into traffic, which certainly could happen, he would not be able to see Jaxon until tomorrow, and he knew he wouldn't get any sleep tonight if he didn't at least start the *discussion* with Cassidy.

But what was he going to say?

Gray knew he wanted to get to know Jaxon, that was irrefutable, but how would he go about it? Would his mother even allow him to spend time with his son? "Probably not without her being there," he said with a touch of bitterness. But then his attitude shifted. Would Cassidy's presence be so bad?

It was then that his thoughts turned back to Hawaii. She had been so beautiful, sitting there on the patio of the hotel lounge. He had spotted her right away but thought that such a beauty would surely be waiting for someone, a husband or fiancée or even just a boyfriend. It could not be possible that she would be there alone. Not someone who looked like her and exuded such sensuality.

But Cassidy had been alone and had even spoken to him, so full of charm and confidence that he'd been taken aback by her. It was a rare occurrence when he was bowled over by someone … anyone. But that was what happened when he had first met her. She had completely taken his breath away. And it had happened again when he saw her on Bainbridge Island.

He had not planned on having sex with Cassidy when he went to the island that day. All he'd wanted was to reconnect with her. Well, he'd wanted to apologize too. Had he done that? Had he said he was sorry for acting like she was a stranger when they saw each other again in his office? He could not remember. All he could remember about that day was her standing there looking sexy as hell. Then the next thing he knew he was kissing her, and she was kissing him back with so much passion that he hadn't been able to think straight.

That was the effect she had on him. Just picturing her in this way caused his body to start reacting and he needed to quickly change his thoughts or suffer the uncomfortable consequences. Gray forced his attention back to his most immediate problem, which was all about one thing, a very real, no holds barred conversation with Cassidy … about their son.

Gray was relieved to see that that it was still ten minutes before eight when he pulled into Cassidy's driveway again. Surely it was still early enough that they could sit down and at least calmly begin a conversation. Hopefully, he would also get a chance to see Jaxon again.

As he walked up to the porch, he noticed that the outside light wasn't on, but he could see from the small, half-circle window at the top of the door that the lights inside the house were. He rang the bell.

Surprised that she was even able to breathe, let alone speak, Cassidy said an almost normal sounding, "Hello, Gray," after opening the door. Her mind was speeding along at about a hundred miles a minute. Why had he come back tonight? What was so important that it couldn't wait until tomorrow? Had he spoken with an attorney already? Or did he just want to talk?

"Hi," Gray said, feeling tongue tied. She was always so lovely, and tonight was no exception, even without makeup and her hair not done to perfection, she was beautiful, maybe even more so.

After a moment of silence Cassidy asked if he wanted to come inside. He nodded and stepped over the threshold. Once she had shut the door, she went into the living room and he followed. "Do you want to sit down?" she asked him.

"I want to …" Gray decided to rephrase his thoughts. He didn't want to start another fight with her and demanding to see Jaxon might do just that. " … May I see Jaxon again?"

Cassidy hesitated but only for a moment. Keeping or trying to keep Jaxon away from him might do more harm than good to their situation. "Sure," she said. "He's in his room, playing." She led the way down the hall. Jaxon was still on the floor with his trucks, moving blocks around and creating a small world on the carpet of his bedroom.

Gray took a deep breath as he laid eyes on the little guy again. And when Jaxon looked up at him while he stood there in the doorway, nearly frozen in place, he felt his heart in his throat. "Hi, Jaxon," he said.

Jaxon looked nervously at his mother. "It's okay, sweetie," she said quietly, stepping into the room. "Mama's right here." The boy went to his mother and wrapped a tiny arm around her leg, but his eyes never left Gray.

"What are you doing, buddy?" Gray asked, not sure exactly how to speak to a child, even though the child was his own flesh and blood.

Jaxon didn't answer, instead he looked up at Cassidy. She smiled and ruffled his hair. "He's building," she said.

Gray looked puzzled. "What do you mean?"

Cassidy moved closer to the blocks. "This," she said, pointing to a clear path. " … is a road and along the road are houses." She then turned to Jaxon and pointed to the block at the end of the street. "What's that, honey?"

"I get slushies there," he said.

"That's right," she told her son. "It's the convenience store around the corner," she explained to Gray. "He does this all the time. He loves building roads and neighborhoods. He does it at the park, he does it in the backyard and right here in his room. He even tried to build a skyscraper tonight but couldn't quite figure out how to get the height without it falling over."

Gray smiled. "You need to start with a stable base," he said, and before Cassidy knew what was happening, he was on the floor with the blocks, laying them out to create a platform. The really amazing thing was that Jaxon let go of her and went over to see what Gray was doing. Before long, he was sitting next to Gray, handing him blocks and watching as the tower grew.

Cassidy's eyes filled with tears as she watched her son play with his father for the first time. Was this the start of something real and good, she wondered? There was still so much to work out, so much to talk about. And it was time for Jaxon to go to bed.

"I hate to break this up," she finally said. "But it's bedtime."

Jaxon stood up. "Go potty," he said to his Mama.

Cassidy took Jaxon by the hand and started for the door.

"I'll wait in the living room," Gray said. "If that's okay?"

Cassidy nodded and looked down at her son. "Do you want to say goodnight to …" she didn't know what to call Gray and she felt very odd about that. He was the boy's father, but was that really something she wanted to try to explain to Jaxon tonight?

Jaxon watched as Gray stood up. "Goodnight," he said.

"Goodnight, Jaxon," Gray said. He then went up the hall to the living room.

It took Cassidy fifteen minutes to join Gray. "I read him a short story tonight," Cassidy said, once she'd entered the living room.

Gray was standing by the sliding glass door looking out at her backyard. In his mind he was designing a playground for Jaxon and this tiny yard simply would not hold all of the things he wanted to put in it. "Please don't vary from your routine on my account," he said as he turned to face her.

"It's fine," she said. "He's in bed now. So … would you like to sit down?"

"Yes," Gray said, really looking around the living room for the first time as he sought out a place to sit. The room was comfortably furnished, with a large couch and matching chair, a coffee table with *kid friendly* rounded corners and edges, two end tables with lamps, only one was lit, and pretty pillows on the couch and chair. The palette of the room was soft greens and light blues with splashes of bright orange in the pillows and rug. Overall, it was a very peaceful room despite there being a box of toys in the corner near the back door, or maybe it was because of the toys? Gray sat in the chair while Cassidy took the couch, pulling her bare feet up under her.

Neither spoke right away and that was because neither knew how to start this conversation. Gray found it odd that he was having such a difficult time with this. Now, had this been a new project or string of hotels he wanted to build where he was negotiating terms, this would have been a piece of cake. But it wasn't. This was about a child, his child, and the mother of his child. Maybe he was having such a hard time because he really didn't know what he wanted. Yes, he knew he wanted to get to know his son better but what about the mother? At one time he'd thought he wanted to pursue a relationship with her, but that had been before he knew she had kept his son from him. Maybe that was where he should start?

"Cassidy, I … ah … I need to know why," he began. "I'm not trying to start an argument with you, but I'd really like to hear why you didn't tell me."

She met his questioning gaze head on. "I wanted to," she told him. "You can't know how much I wanted to. And that was actually my first thought when you turned around that day in your office and I saw that it was you standing there. Good gosh, Gray, I've thought of nothing else for the last four years. Do you know that I even tried to find you when I found out I was pregnant?"

Gray showed surprise. "You did?"

"Yes, but the only place I knew where to begin looking was the hotel in Hawaii," she explained. "They were no help."

"Why not?" he asked.

"Well, Mr. Jensen …"

"Oh, yeah."

"Without a last name, even if they were so inclined to help, which they weren't, I couldn't give them any correct information," she said. "I had no idea who you really were."

Gray was sitting with his elbows on the arms of the chair. He had made a fist with his right hand and had wrapped his left hand around his right. He'd been holding both up in front of his mouth. He now dropped his head and began bumping his forehead with his fists. "So, stupid," were his words, sounding like a groan to Cassidy.

"Gray?" Cassidy asked.

He looked up at her. "I must have picked up my phone 20 dozen times to have my private investigator find you," he told her. "I think I already told you that when we were together that day on Bainbridge. I wish like hell that I had."

"So do I, Gray," Cassidy said.

"Speaking of Bainbridge," he said tentatively. "Why didn't you tell me then?"

Cassidy looked away from him with her cheeks flushing. "Should I have said something before, during or after our little …?" She didn't finish the sentence and that was because she didn't know what to politely call their encounter.

Gray smiled mischievously. "Well …" he said while a huge grin spread itself all over his handsome face.

Cassidy gave him a, *you've-got-to-be-kidding* look. "I was going to tell you on the ferry," she said. "I even started to."

"I knew you were keeping something from me," Gray told her.

She nodded. "I felt like I needed more time to get to know you better. Can you understand that?" When Gray didn't respond she took that as a no and continued. "Gray, the only things I knew about you for sure were that you are an incredibly successful businessman and that we're great in bed together. I knew nothing about your personal life, where you live, who your friends are, did you have family, had you been married before. You were, or are, almost a complete stranger to me. My son …"

"Our son," Gray interjected, speaking a little testily.

"You're right," she said, just as testily. "But I'm the only parent he knows. I'm his entire family. I take care of him, I feed and clothe him, I comfort him when he wakes up crying at night because of a bad dream and I kiss his tears away when he's skinned his knee. Where were you? Spain?"

"That's not fair," he said. "I didn't know about him."

"And why is that, Gray?"

He looked away from her. It was true and he had to face it. He was the one with the means and the ability to find her, if he'd chosen to. Why hadn't he? "I know, Cass," he said. "This is all my fault."

"No, Gray, that's not what I'm saying," Cassidy said. "I'm not blaming you for what happened in the past. I didn't have to go to bed with you in Hawaii … I wanted to. And now we have a son to think about." She paused for a moment to collect her thoughts. "Would you like something to drink? I know I'd like some water."

"Yes," he said with a nod. "Water would be great."

When she returned from the kitchen with two glasses, Cassidy knew exactly what she wanted to say next. "That's all I've been doing, Gray, thinking about Jaxon and what's best for him."

"So, you think living without a father is what's best for him?" Gray said, stunned and worried by her words.

"As a matter of fact," she told him. "No, I don't think that at all. I would love for him to have a warm, loving father … and not a father figure but a real, honest to goodness dad. I want a man who is going to spend time with him, taking him to the park and to ball games, someone who will be at his soccer games and parent teacher conferences. I want someone who can't wait to take him camping and canoeing."

"I don't know anything about camping or canoeing," Gray said, somewhat baffled by her comments.

Cassidy smiled. "Neither do I, but I think you get my point."

They both sat in silence contemplating for a few moments. Cassidy was still wondering what Gray was doing there now. At times he still seemed angry with her and yet, he also seemed like he was trying to understand her and what she had done. Was this solely about Jaxon? Was this only about getting to know his son?

Gray felt that he was starting to understand Cassidy a little better. She was obviously a good mother, but … and that was where he was now. A tiny yet huge *but* lingered between them, last night, her not wanting to see him anymore, and not giving him the opportunity to meet his son. Yes, she was looking out for Jaxon's welfare, *but* without Gray being given the chance to meet his son, how would she ever understand what kind of father he would be?

"Last night you said you didn't want to see me anymore," he finally said. "Was that to keep me from Jaxon, or from you, or what? I don't understand."

"When I mentioned family and I asked if you wanted one of your own, you became Gray Griffin, international business-man," she explained. "You told me you were too busy. Where did that leave me or Jaxon? Especially him. And while I didn't want to end up being another Terri to you, running into you and another woman somewhere after you've just returned from another one of your several year's absences, I'm an adult and though it would hurt, it wouldn't be the end of my life. I've already lived through it. But what about Jaxon? What about the feelings that he would undoubtedly develop for you? Let's say you did get to know him, and you spent time with him, even taking him for weekends and such. But then a project comes up in the South of France or South Africa, what then? What about Jaxon's feelings for you? Are you going to fly clear back to Seattle for your weekend with him?"

"Yes," Gray said with a *matter of fact* tone in his voice.

"And what if there's a problem on the site that needs your attention?" Cassidy asked, playing devil's advocate. "Will you put him off, or will you hold the job? One would have to suffer, which would it be?"

"I could exchange weekends with you," he said.

"Not if it's the big game."

"What do you mean?"

"I have no idea what Jaxon's interests are going be when he gets older," Cassidy said. "But what if its soccer and what if he is in a championship game the same weekend your project needs you the most? What if it's the science fair? What if it's high school graduation or the night of his high school play or even his prom? All of those things are so important, Gray. I know where I'm going to be and what I'm going to be doing, do you?"

"Look, Cass, I don't have all the answers yet—"

"And neither do I," she said, interrupting him. "I'm just trying to explain why I did what I did last night, where my thought processes took me and why. At that moment, when we were talking, the whole situation just seemed so insurmountable."

Gray thought about all the things Cassidy had laid out. Was this situation impossible? "I could take him with me," Gray offered. "He could see the world and learn about different cultures."

Cassidy heart sank. Was this where they were heading? The six-month split? And how would she live for six months of the year without her precious boy? Or would Gray petition the court for even more? Were her worst fears actually coming true? A tear escaped from the corner of her eye and rolled down her cheek.

Gray noticed a tear on Cassidy's cheek and wondered why she was crying. He'd thought that she wanted him to come up with solutions. "What's wrong?" he asked, doing his best to offer solace when he truly did not grasp her sudden emotional upheaval.

Cassidy wanted to jump up, run down the hall, get Jaxon and disappear. She wanted to go someplace new and start over with her son, someplace that no one would ever find them. Was there such a place? She didn't really think so. A sob rose in her throat and flew out between her lips before she could stop it. "I can't," she wailed. "Don't you see I can't just give him to you!"

Gray was stunned. "What?" he asked, sitting up straight. "What are you talking about?"

"Jaxon," she sobbed. "I can't … I won't give him to you!"

"I don't expect you to give him to me," Gray said, striving for as much passion as he heard in her wails. And then all at once it became clear to him, as if a light bulb had just gone on in his head. Her greatest fear, her reason for not telling him about Jaxon, subconsciously or otherwise, was that he was somehow going to try to take Jaxon away from her. He slid from the chair to the couch and folded her into his arms. "Oh, Cass," he said hoarsely. "Is that what you've been afraid of?"

She fell against him and nodded.

"I would never …" He was choked up as well. He tried clearing his throat but still had to wait a minute before speaking again. He sat her up straight and looked directly into her eyes. "Look at me," he told her, and she did, meeting his gaze with big, wet eyes. "I would never, ever, under any circumstances try to take Jaxon away from you. I can see what a wonderful mother you are."

"But you said you'd take him with you if you left the country," she said, still afraid of what he could do if he chose.

"Not without his mother," he said with a smile. "And certainly not while he was in school. I was thinking of summer breaks and holidays. But only if you said it was okay and if you could come too."

Cassidy needed a tissue desperately. "I'll be right back," she said with a sniff. She got up and went to her bedroom where she knew a box stood on her nightstand. After she was done blowing her nose and wiping her tears away, she left her room and was surprised to find Gray in the hallway. He was standing at Jaxon's door and peeking in at him.

"He looks so—" Gray started to say.

"Like he'd never do anything wrong?" Cassidy asked. "Like an angel?"

"Yes," Gray agreed. "Just like an angel."

Without thinking, Cassidy put her arm around Gray's back and peeked into the room as well. "I've often sat in his room and just watched him sleep," she told him. "When I'm irritated about something, or stressed over work, it somehow gives me comfort and peace."

"I can see that," Gray said to her, feeling her arm around him and realizing how good it felt. "I guess we should go back to the living room."

"Yes," Cassidy said, as she finally realized where her arm was. "Oh, sorry," she said, letting her arm drop.

"Don't be," Gray said. "I didn't mind … at all."

They returned to the living room, but this time with Gray also seated on the couch, inches from where she was sitting.

"I think I'm beginning to understand, Cass," he said, speaking first, and he really believed what he was saying. "You were afraid I'd try to take him once I found out that he was mine. And you were trying to get to know me better to see if I was capable of doing something like that. What you think you found out last night is that I'm not interested in having a family. Does that about sum it up?"

Cassidy nodded. "Pretty much. Look, I know I was wrong to not tell you, regardless of my fears, but a few minutes ago when you said you would take him with you if you left the country, my very first thought was to grab him and run. I could never afford to fight you in court and if I lost him now, I think I'd just lie down and die."

Gray's anger toward Cassidy had completely dissipated. She was the mother bear protecting her cub. He could not hate her and certainly couldn't blame her for only looking out for that beautiful little person down the hall. He would probably have done the same if it had been him in her situation. He looked into her big blue eyes and what he saw there was love, overwhelming love for a child … his child. Could she ever love him like that? He thought about his next words very carefully before he spoke, but when he did, he was absolutely sure about them.

"I know what I said last night about being too busy with work to have a family," he began. "And at one time that was true. I actually think I buried myself in work to avoid entanglements. Then I met you and for the first time in my life I thought about what it would be like to have a home and kids and all of that. I think that's why I didn't try to find you. I think I was afraid of feeling something I never had before. But now … I don't want to go back to being alone, Cass, and I don't want to live without getting to know my son. And if you want me to learn how to camp and go canoeing, then that's what I'll do."

As he spoke, uttering such beautiful words, Cassidy felt as though her heart was filling, overflowing with joy, so much so that she was sure it would burst at any moment. "Oh, Gray," she said with a joyous laugh. "You don't have to go canoeing!"

epilogue

2021

Cassidy sat on the open patio of The Grand Hawaiian Hotel and Resort in Wailea, Maui. She was enjoying the fabulous view she had of the ocean, the aroma of nearby flowers and a light, soft breeze. It was a little over four years since her first visit to this incredibly beautiful place and, in a way, that night, that one perfect night, was when her life had really begun. She couldn't help smiling as she thought of what had brought her here this time.

After an hours-long conversation between her and Gray regarding Jaxon that night at her house after he had found out about the boy, they had turned their attention to each other. Cassidy could still laugh out loud when she thought about Gray telling her that he would learn the ins and outs of camping and operating a canoe if that was what it would take to be with them. It wasn't, of course, what she had hoped to convey, but once she'd explained that all she wanted was someone who was going to be there for both her and their son, he'd smiled and said, "That would be my pleasure."

"You know, you could really make a girl fall in love with you," Cassidy had told him.

"That sounds so great," he'd said in return, speaking in such an emotional tone his eyes had misted over. "Because I believe that I'm falling in love with you all over again."

"What do you mean … again?" she had asked, with her heartbeat increasing tenfold, or so it felt, which made her breathless.

"I think I fell in love with you the minute you suggested that we pretend to be a couple named Jensen," he'd explained. "Remember?"

"Of course, I remember. Gray, I remember every single minute of that night. But it took me a little longer to fall in love," she had teased. "I didn't fall in love with you until you asked me to dance on the beach. Then I was a goner."

And now, here she was again, at the same table, on the same patio, in the same hotel where it all began. Would tonight end differently than it had the last time she was here? Or would she end up in another incredibly handsome man's bed?

Cassidy's breath caught in her throat as she saw him step out onto the patio. He was tall with a slender but muscular build and dark, sandy blonde hair. He had light eyes and a smile that could light up a room. The best part was that he was staring directly at her. Did he want to sit in the empty chair she had at her table? She smiled and waved him over.

"Any problems?" she asked, as the man approached.

"No, we've got it all under control," he answered.

"Mama!" Jaxon said, as he was lowered to her arms. "We went potty."

"Good boy," Cassidy said, as she kissed his little cheek. "And what about Daddy?"

"Yes, Daddy's a good boy too," Jaxon answered.

"Then I think Daddy deserves a kiss also."

"I would agree with that," Gray said, as he bent to get his kiss. "So, what do we want for dinner?"

"I think there's only one thing we can have," Cassidy said with huge grin. "Fish tacos."

"Are you sure you don't want to go to the Seafood restaurant in the hotel?" Gray asked. "They also have a really nice steakhouse."

Cassidy shook her head. "No way, I've been craving these tacos since the last time I was here."

Gray helped her up from her chair and each of them took one of Jaxon's hands. They walked through the lobby and out the front door on their way to Maui's Fresh Catch. "Do you think this will end up being another perfect night?" Cassidy asked with a loving glance at her man.

"Nope," Gray told her.

Cassidy frowned at him. "Why not?" she asked. "This is our honeymoon, after all."

He smiled. "Because I think what we're heading for now is …" He hesitated, or rather, he paused to let this moment saturate each of their senses. And then he completed his sentence with what they both believed to be the most wonderful truth of their lives. " … one perfect life."

They laughed together, swung their precious son just enough to lift his tiny feet from the ground for a moment, causing him to laugh joyously, they began walking again, heading out, as Gray had just announced, forward, into their one perfect life, only Cassidy silently added one very important word, *together*. One perfect life … *together*. One perfect family.

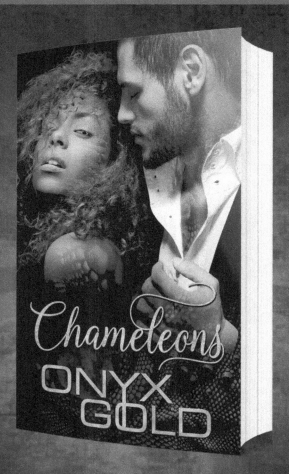

COMING
SOON

CayellePublishing.com

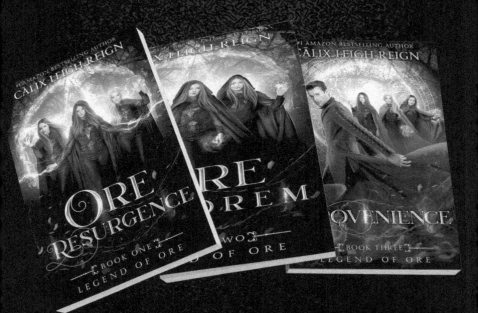

MORE READS

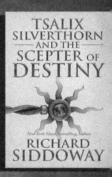

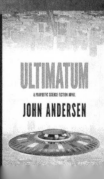